Also by the Author:

Memoirs of an Angel—Just because you had a bad past
doesn't mean you can't have a great future.

Coming soon:
Forgotten Heroes—Everyone deserves to come home.
The Christmas Express—The best gifts come from the heart.
The Conscience Fund—Money can't buy everything.
Withersake—The descent into darkness.

FOOTPRINTS

Angels Are Real—Some Even Have Fur

Jim Huggins

Archway Publishing books may be ordered through booksellers or by contacting:

Archway Publishing
1663 Liberty Drive
Bloomington, IN 47403
www.archwaypublishing.com
1 (888) 242-5904

Scriptures taken from the Holy Bible, New International Version®, NIV®. Copyright © 1973, 1978, 1984, 2011 by Biblica, Inc.™ Used by permission of Zondervan. All rights reserved worldwide. www.zondervan.com The "NIV" and "New International Version" are trademarks registered in the United States Patent and Trademark Office by Biblica, Inc.™

Adaption from screenplay by Terry Burns.

ISBN: 978-1-4808-8062-7 (sc)
ISBN: 978-1-4808-8061-0 (e)

Library of Congress Control Number: 2019910111

Print information available on the last page.

Archway Publishing rev. date: 08/19/2019

For Cadie

Sometimes losing everything leads to something
greater than you could ever dream of.

CONTENTS

PROLOGUE

Nearly three thousand years ago, a man named Elijah served God as a prophet. His reputation as a man of God grew in a land where few believed in the one, true God. Yet, even with all his victories in the Lord, Elijah allowed the threats of one person to shatter his hopes for the future.

Elijah became discouraged and fled. Wanting to hide from everyone, including God, Elijah gave up. He cried out, "Lord, I have had enough! Take my life!" God saw this and knew Elijah had a greater purpose. He was patient with His servant and allowed him to rest.

Then, God sent an angel to appear before Elijah. And the angel said, "Arise!"

Elijah learned that journeys begin one step at a time. His journey demonstrates that in every life there comes a defining moment. A moment when everything changes. Often, it's a point in time when things appear dark and grim, perhaps even hopeless. The person is then irrevocably transformed by the light of faith, hope, and conviction.

For David Hyler and a German shepherd named Cadie, that moment began when they met each other. Theirs is a stunning story of hope and love, of rescue and redemption—not only for themselves, but for the countless others whose lives they touched.

But to tell of their transformation, and to experience the wonder and miracle for yourself, we must go back to where the story first began.

ONE

SUMMER 1967

FIVE-YEAR-OLD DAVID SAT in the driveway playing with Ginger, his beloved stuffed dog, oblivious to his father's muted cursing and the clanging of the tools emanating from the garage.

On the other side of the building, his father, Gerald Hyler, struggled to repair a lawn tractor, his lack of success escalating his temper rapidly. Gerald stood up and wiped sweat from his forehead with the back of a greasy hand and onto his filthy T-shirt. "Will, get out here! Now!" he bellowed in the general direction of the aging white house.

The heat and the humidity were taking their toll on David's father as he glared at the offending piece of machinery. When it dawned on him that his older son wasn't coming, he yelled louder. "William, I said for you to get out here! Right now!"

Gerald stalked around the garage and spotted his younger son. "Where's your brother?"

David smiled and pointed across the street. "He's playing with his friends."

Gerald sighed deeply. "Just what I need." He grimaced. "Well, you'll have to do. Come over here, and be quick about it."

With childlike innocence, David, missing the danger signs of his father's anger, followed behind him, glad to have a chance to be a helper for once. It was always his brother, Will, who got to help, so this would be a special treat.

"Yay! I'm going to help Daddy," David said happily to Ginger. "And I'm going to be the best helper ever."

The boy raced to stand beside his father, who disdainfully studied the disabled mower sitting amid half-mown grass at the rear of the backyard. He ran his hand through his short-cropped hair, depositing more grease and dirt there. Looking down at David, he muttered "I guess you aren't strong enough to hold this up while I fix it. I'll have to find another way."

Gerald was the kind of man who, as a rule, didn't have the patience to work on things. He grew frustrated easily, and his close-to-the-surface temper soon made whatever project he was working on more difficult, if not impossible. Added to that, in this instance, his work was interrupted when he ran over a piece of cable, which wrapped around the twin blades of the mower and locked it down tight. That alone had pushed his emotions close to the boiling-over point.

After carrying two cinder blocks out to the mower, Gerald found a long board he could use as a lever to lift the side of the machine. He positioned the blocks close to the mower and inserted the board. He looked over at his small son, who was watching with great interest. "Get over here," he ordered. With one swift motion, Gerald grabbed David under the armpits and plopped him none too gently on the end of the board, as if making him walk the plank, but from a seated position. It raised the front of the lawn tractor sufficiently off the ground. He pointed a finger in the boy's face and barked, "Sit still. You're gonna hold this up. Don't you move!"

David smiled shyly. He would do anything to please his dad, and it had always been that way. Besides having her light-brown hair and soft brown eyes, he also shared other attributes with his mother, Katherine—her gentle nature, her quick smile, her desire to make everyone, especially her husband, happy.

David's brother, Will, was more like his dad.

Gerald crawled under the mower deck and began to work. The cutters he was using didn't make any headway on the heavy wire.

David fidgeted with Ginger in his hands, swinging his legs back and forth, causing the mower to move slightly. Exasperated, Gerald slid out from under the mower deck, got to his feet, and stomped over to David. He jerked the stuffed animal away from his son and tossed it aside. "Boy, I told you not to move!"

David froze. The vehemence in his father's voice scared him. He hated it when his father got angry. Bad things always happened soon after.

Gerald crawled back under the mower and continued to wrestle with the repair. A minute later, the cutters he was using got away from him and bounced out from under the mower. David jumped down to get them.

The mower slammed down, barely giving Gerald time to get out of the way.

David walked over to his dad and held out the wire cutters. "Here, Daddy, I got these for you."

David saw his dad's anger boil over as he jerked the tool from the boy's hand. "I told you not to move, and I meant it. Can't you do anything right? All you had to do was to sit still. How hard is that?"

David erupted in tears. "I'm sorry, Daddy. I was just trying to help."

Towering over his son, Gerald continued to berate him, yelling and cursing, ignoring the boy's sobbing apologies. "You could have killed me." His eyes narrowed. "Here, I'll show you. This could have happened to me." His face a mask of rage mere inches from David's face, Gerald grabbed the stuffed dog and ripped the head off.

Staring in shock at his treasured toy, David began to scream and cry uncontrollably.

Gerald threw the decapitated toy aside. "Take that infernal noise out of here. I don't have time for it. You're useless!" Returning his attention to the mower, he muttered under his breath, "Worthless kid," and slung the tool he was holding across the yard. Then, realizing he needed the tool, he cursed and went to retrieve it.

David scooped up his toy and ran for the house. "Mommy! Mommy!" He ran straight for his bedroom and threw himself on his bed.

His mother raced in to him. "David, what is it?"

He looked up at her, eyes filled with tears, and held out the decapitated animal. Ginger was his favorite companion. She was more of a security blanket than a stuffed toy.

His mother sat on the bed beside him. "My, my. What happened to this?"

"Daddy."

"Daddy did this?" David's mother stroked his head. "Don't you worry. I'll fix your puppy. She'll be good as new."

Just then, the engine of the lawn tractor revved in the yard, and the sound moved closer to the house.

David's mom got up. "You rest now, honey. I have to go make dinner. I'll come get you when it's ready."

Katherine moved quietly from David's bedside to the door leading to the hall. She paused and glanced back at her son, her face a mixture of warring emotions ranging from worry to anger as well as fear. She turned away and walked down the hall to the kitchen trying to mentally prepare herself for the battle she knew was about to occur.

As she entered the kitchen, Gerald came in the back door, slamming the screen behind him. She moved to the cabinet, removed some utensils, and began to prepare dinner. He ignored her and went to the sink to fill a glass with water. Katherine stared at his sweat-stained, greasy back. His face and neck were flushed. All were signs of the anger she knew so well. She knew it wasn't time to cross him, but in spite of her fear, she knew she had to defend her son. Busying herself opening a can of green beans, she said in a quiet voice, "You were too harsh on David."

He didn't even bother to turn when he addressed her. "If he isn't treated like a baby, he won't grow up to be one," he said matter-of-factly.

Abandoning the act of preparing the meal, she put the back of her hand to her forehead in frustration. "He's only five, Gerald. You expect him to be like William, but he can't be. It's not fair for you to ask him to be like his older brother. If you keep beating him down, he'll never grow up."

Pivoting viciously toward her, he spat out, "And if you keep treating him like he's God's gift to the world, his big brother will do the beating instead."

"Me?" She clasped her hand to her chest. Her voice rose. "You're the one turning William against his younger brother! How dare you—"

He jabbed his finger at her, raising his voice to be heard over her objections. "How dare *I*? He can't do anything right, and you tell him everything is okay. How dare *you*."

He turned his back on her. Then, after a few moments' silence, he swiveled his head in her direction. His voice was softer but still full of menace. "How dare you stand there and preach to me about how to raise my sons."

Gerald threw his glass toward the sink, shattering it, and stormed past Katherine and out of the room. A moment later, she heard the mower's engine start as Gerald continued his task of mowing the yard.

Fighting tears unsuccessfully, Katherine went to get the dustpan and broom. After she swept up the broken glass, she stumbled to the kitchen table. Hanging her head, she began to weep silently.

She was exhausted. It was just too much. It had been too much for a long time, but she was trapped. Trapped in a loveless, abusive marriage. Trapped by her love for both her sons, especially her sensitive younger son, David.

A silent observer to the ongoing chaos, David stood in the doorway and watched his mother cry, tears on his own cheeks as well.

SEPTEMBER 1967

Gerald drove into the driveway in his old Ford Fairlane. Katherine watched from the porch as he got out and opened the door. Two young German shepherd pups bounded from the car. They had dark coats, gangly long legs, and boundless energy. As they scampered past the porch where she stood, she stepped down and raised an eyebrow at Gerald. "Pups?"

He nodded. "Pups."

"For the children?" she asked, concerned.

The smile on his face faded. Gerald didn't have discussions. He lectured or ordered. "Of course, for the children. I had dogs when I was a kid. It's just what they need to teach them responsibility. We've been through this already."

Gerald pushed past her and followed the pups to the backyard, where the boys were playing. "Hey, boys!" he called. "Look what I have."

The boys came running.

Katherine frowned as she came around the corner. "Are you sure this is a good idea?" She folded her arms across her chest. "I mean, Will is certainly old enough, but I think David is too young. A dog is a big responsibility, and that pup will grow up much faster than he does."

Gerald didn't take his eyes off the boys. "I said that we're getting the boys their own dogs. End ... of ... discussion." He walked away, leaving her staring at the ground in frustration.

Katherine turned her attention toward David as he hugged one of the puppies. She sighed. She knew he'd wanted a dog for a long time and spent his days imagining his stuffed dog was real. Will had also talked about having a dog, which only made David want a dog more. David so much wanted to be like his brother.

Katherine smiled. Maybe she was wrong. Maybe David was old enough.

"Hey, boys," Gerald said, "what are you going to name them?"

Will didn't hesitate. "Laddie."

David responded, "Lassie."

Will frowned at his little brother. "You're just copying me. That's a silly name for a boy dog."

"It is not."

The bickering continued for a few minutes before the boys turned their attention back to the pups. When Will began throwing a ball, his pup went after it with enthusiasm.

Katherine could tell David's pup wanted to run after the ball too. He'd watched it when it was thrown, and now was squirming and jumping around trying to get out of a hug that had become a heartfelt headlock. David was clearly happy with his newfound friend, and she began to relax as they frolicked. And even though this puppy was nearly as big as David, her fears gave way to thankfulness. Perhaps she worried too much, she thought, and turned back toward the house.

An instant later, the eager-to-play pup jumped up on David, knocking him down and landing on him. David screamed and started to cry. At first, the pup cowered nearby at the noise, staring a David. It then raced to join Will and the other pup.

"Mommy, Mommy, take it away," David cried as she ran toward him. "It hurt me. I don't want it."

Crouching down, she peered at the small scratch on his cheek.

Gerald grabbed the dog up harshly and headed back to the car. After putting the dog back in the car, he slammed the door and muttered, "Worthless kid. He's such a baby."

David's eyes got wide as his mother sat beside him in the grass, cuddling him. In a voice just above a whisper her said, "No, wait—I didn't mean it. Please bring Lassie back."

But there was an immediate slam of a car door, and then the starting of the Fairlane's engine. Loose gravel flew everywhere as Gerald drove off with the pup.

David glanced up tearfully. "I didn't mean it, Mommy. Please bring him back."

"I know, sweetheart, but I can't. It's too late. You know your father."

David buried his head in her shoulder and cried.

"There, there," Katherine said soothingly. "Someday you will have your own dog, and it will be a very special dog. I promise. You'll see."

Her words were meant to soothe his pain. Unfortunately, they provided little comfort.

OCTOBER 1967, 8:00 A.M.

They were at it again. David huddled in his bedroom, listening to his mom and dad argue.

"Can't you see how bad that fog is? Look out the window! You can't even see your garden ten feet away." Gerald said. "You don't need to be out in it, especially to drive as far as Charlotte."

Katherine was undeterred. "We need new draperies, and this is the last day of the sale."

"What's wrong with the draperies we have?"

"Don't you want our home to look nice? We've had these drapes for—"

"I don't care." He gestured at the window. "It's nasty out, and I don't want you driving in that weather. The drapes are just fine! I work hard for my money, and all you do is work hard to spend it. I swear, you'll be spending my money till the day you die." He stomped to the door and jerked it open. "Stay home! You hear me?" He slammed the door behind him.

David heard his dad stomp down the stairs that led to the garage. A moment later, the car door slammed, and the engine started, followed by the tires squealing as his dad pulled out of the drive and headed to work.

From the window, Katherine watched her husband's angry exit, and then she turned to prepare David's breakfast.

Still in his pajamas, David stood in the darkened doorway. "Mommy, do you really have to go?"

"Yes, sweetie. We've needed draperies for a long time, and this is the only day I can go. I'll be back this afternoon. I promise."

"Can I go with you?"

"Not this time."

"What if Daddy's right?"

"Right about what?"

"That it isn't safe to go."

Katherine sighed, sat at the table, and drew David onto her lap. "I don't want you to worry about that. I'll be fine. Your grandmommy is coming to pick you up. You'll have fun. You can draw a picture for me, and I'll frame it and hang it on the wall."

David smiled. "G'anny's picking me up?" He had trouble with the letter *r*.

"That's right. How about that?" She grinned.

"Okay." David loved his grandmother, Kate, and always enjoyed spending time with her.

Katherine hugged him close. "It's just a day trip," she said reassuringly, hugging him even tighter. "Now you remember: I love you more than anything. I'd never, ever leave you."

"Promise?"

She smiled, kissed his cheek, and said, "I promise!" Then, she reached behind her. "Oh, and by the way, I have someone to keep you company while I'm gone."

"Ginger!" David hugged the stuffed animal to him.

"Yes, and good as new. I fixed her for you last night."

He gave her a big hug. "You're the best mommy in the whole world."

As if on cue, the doorbell rang, and it was time for David to begin his adventures with his g'anny. Katherine smiled as she watched him run to answer the door, already thinking about hurrying back home later today to experience her own special greeting from David.

9:20 A.M.

An hour or so later, Katherine was having second thoughts as she drove toward Charlotte. The fog was much thicker than she'd first realized. Perhaps she should have listened to her husband, but the way he bulldozed over her in everything just made her so mad. Sometimes the need to assert herself was overpowering.

It will be all right, she told herself. She reduced her speed appropriately and clicked her headlights down to low beam, where they wouldn't bounce back in her face so much. The fog was a thick blanket that deadened sound. It was quiet; so very quiet that she turned the radio on for company. When rain mixed with the fog, she clicked on the wipers, the rhythmic *swipe-click, swipe-click* keeping time with the music as she sang along softly.

From her husband's lectures, Katherine was aware that roads had a layer of scum on them that wasn't noticeable when they were dry, but that could become very slick in the rain. She moved the wheel a little one way and then the other as a test to make sure the car had sufficient traction. It seemed all right.

9:30 A.M.

By the odometer reading, she calculated she was still some thirty miles from Charlotte—not that she could tell by looking out the window. Passing scenery was hidden in the spooky whiteness of the fog. Up close to the road, trees stood out like ghostly sentinels as she passed. It made an eerie picture, filling her with an unexpected feeling of dread.

9:51 A.M.

It only took an instant for Katherine's world to change.

The blazing red of a stoplight suddenly exploded out of the fog. Conditioned by years of driving experience, she reacted, stomping hard on the brake. The car began to slide as the tires fought to keep a grip on the slick road. Katherine fought to turn in the direction of the skid, just as she'd been taught, and the car corrected itself. She came to a stop perfectly.

"Whew!" she exclaimed. "That was close!"

9:52 A.M.

The next set of lights were bright white and came from out of nowhere. There was no time to scream.

3:00 P.M.

It was raining gently as David lay on the floor of the porch, drawing with his crayons. His grandmother, Kate, sat nearby, knitting. David loved his grandmother, a petite woman with white hair and a gentle disposition. If David couldn't be with his mom, this was the place he most wanted to be.

A minute later, Kate got up and walked to the edge of the porch. Hands on her hips, she yelled at Will, who was perched on a low branch in a tree in the front yard. "Will! Get down out of that tree."

"It's not raining under here," Will shot back.

She harrumphed, then ordered, "You get out of that tree right now. You never know when lightning might take a notion to strike in weather like this."

As Will jumped down, a police car pulled up to the curb.

"Somebody's coming," Will called.

Kate edged over to the steps as the officer exited the car. Her concern escalated as her pastor's car pulled up behind the patrol car. The combination of the two was never good.

The pastor got out, opened his umbrella, and joined the police officer.

"David, keep working on your drawing," she said with far more confidence than she was feeling. "I have to go talk to these men."

"Okay, G'anny."

Her legs abruptly feeling like lead, but she walked slowly toward the two men who had stopped at the edge of the sidewalk. "Pastor. Officer," she said in greeting, then asked the question she didn't want to: "What's wrong?"

Pastor Burke made room for her under his umbrella. He had his "professional" face on, she noted. "Sorry to make you come out in the rain, Kate," he said, "but I thought it best to wait out of the hearing of the boys."

Kate remained frozen in time. The pause lasted far too long. It always did with bad news. "What's happened?"

"Kate, there's no easy way to tell you," the pastor said. "It's Katherine. Her car was hit by a huge dump truck full of rock and gravel. She was killed instantly."

"Oh no." A single groan escaped her throat. Her hand reached out, and her legs buckled, as if she were looking for a place to sit. The men took her arm to steady her. Katherine was Kate's only child. She didn't seem to be able to comprehend what she was hearing. She didn't seem to be able to get her breath, and she reached her left hand up to her throat, as if her heart were there and she could stop it from hurting.

Trying to collect herself, she glanced over at her grandsons. Will was watching, the signs of worry and concern clearly showing on his face. David remained in his imaginary world created by crayons.

"Oh no," Kate said again softly.

"Let me help you to the porch where you can sit down," the pastor suggested.

She held up a hand. "No, wait. Give me a moment." She struggled to pull herself together, to focus. "I can't scare the boys. It must be broken to them gently." Her hands shook as she fought to regain control. She took several deep breaths. "I just can't wrap my mind around it, but I have to do this. I simply have to be strong for them."

"Yes, ma'am. I understand."

A stray thought struck. "Does Gerald know?"

"He was out of the office. We're trying to reach him."

Pastor Burke retained his grip on her arm. "What do you need me to do, Kate?"

"Can you help me tell the boys?"

"Of course." He looked at the two. "Given the difference in their ages, they should be told separately. How about if I take Will for a little walk, and you sit down with David?"

"Yes, I think that's a good idea."

The officer turned to leave, saying, "I'll try to track down your son-in-law."

"Let me walk you to the porch," Pastor Burke said.

Kate took a deep breath, steeling herself to do what must be done. *How do you say something like this gently?* she wondered. She didn't know, but she had to figure it out. She began walking back to the porch.

By now, David had stopped coloring and saw what was happening at the end of the driveway. He was very worried. He knew from experience that it wasn't a good thing when adults whispered. He wondered what he'd done to get into trouble. But if he was in trouble, he was certainly not in a hurry to find out about it.

Still, he couldn't help but watch as the pastor put his arm around Will's shoulder and led him down the sidewalk, talking quietly. Halfway down the walk, Will pivoted to stare at the older man. David saw shock on his brother's face. Will's shoulders then began to shake as the pastor embraced him.

Maybe I can do something to make it all better, David thought. So, he smiled brightly at his grandmother as she stepped onto the porch. He held up the drawing he'd been working on. "Look what I drew." There was no response.

Now David knew something was very wrong. "G'anny, what is it?"

"Oh, baby." She broke into tears.

David jumped up and wrapped his arms around her. He didn't understand why she wouldn't answer. "G'anny?"

She was silent for a long time, then just blurted out, "David, your mommy is not coming back."

He frowned. "I don't understand. She said she would never leave me."

There was another pause, and his grandmother said softly, "Sometimes things happen that are not up to us."

"But she'll come back later, right?"

She shook her head. "No, David. She's never coming back."

David stood frozen, unable to understand the simple words from G'anny. It was too much to take in. His mom had promised.

The artwork slipped from his hands and fell to the floor. It was a picture of David and his mom holding hands.

4:30 P.M.

The police officer found Gerald Hyler's car outside a diner. He entered to find Gerald sitting alone with a cup of coffee in front of him.

"Mr. Hyler?"

Evidently lost in thought, Gerald didn't even look up. He just stared at his coffee. "What?" When he finally looked up, his eyes were filled with suspicion. "What is it?"

The officer held his hat in his hands and twisted the brim. "May I sit down? I have something to tell you."

Suspicion gave way to concern. Looking back at his coffee, Gerald took a sip and motioned to the seat across from him. "What is it?"

The officer sat down. "It's your wife, sir."

"My wife? What has she done now?" Gerald barked.

"Nothing, sir." The officer paused and waited for Gerald to make eye contact with him. "There's been an accident. She's been killed."

Gerald dismissed the ridiculous news. "An accident? What are you talking about? She's at home."

The officer's silence and unflinching expression suddenly hit Gerald. His reluctant concern now became sheer disbelief. "Where?"

"On the highway to Charlotte. She was hit by a dump truck." The officer paused briefly. In an attempt to soften the news, he added, "She never knew what hit her."

The all-too-familiar rage built once again. Gerald narrowed his eyes. "Charlotte?!" He looked down and stared into the depths of his murky coffee. "So she went, even after I told her not to," he said quietly to no one in particular.

"Sir?"

"Nothing." Gerald fought to stay calm. How could she have disobeyed him?

"Is there anything I can do for you, sir?" the officer asked. "Someone I can call for you?"

Gerald did not respond. Reality was setting in. *How could she have done this to me? Now what?*

"Sir, is there anyone I can call for you?" the officer asked again.

Gerald muttered absently, "Call? What for?"

"I don't know, sir," the officer stammered. "I'm just trying to be helpful."

Keeping his expression as blank as a piece of paper, Gerald looked up at the officer. "You've been helpful. You told me." He resumed his fascination with the cup of coffee. His tone left no doubt the conversation was over.

"Yes, sir. My condolences for your loss."

The officer stood, put his hat on, and walked out.

Alone with his thoughts, Gerald's fears raged to the foreground to join the anger already there. Fears besieged him ... fears he'd never allow anyone to see. Fears that he was alone in life again. Fears that he now had two children to deal with, on top of everything else. And one of them was totally incapable of doing anything for himself.

How could she do this to me? What have I done to deserve this? Now what do I do? Gerald pushed his coffee cup aside.

Out of habit, the waitress refilled the cup as she walked by, but he didn't touch it again.

THREE DAYS LATER

For a child, a funeral can be a very confusing thing, especially with a room full of adults showing a wide range of emotions. They didn't quite register on a youngster struggling to wrap his head around the fact that his mother was gone. Well-intended words were said, but they didn't help. People came to "share the grief," as they said, in whatever way they could. A relative sitting with David wanted to take him up to see his mother, saying that he "could say good-bye and get some closure."

David had no idea what the man meant. Halfway down the aisle, David broke free. He didn't want to see his mother in that box. He didn't want to say good-bye. He only wanted his grandmother—the only safe person left in his world—and didn't understand why others were caring for him while G'anny was sitting up front, crying so hard.

He escaped down the hall to sit alone in the church parlor.

Gerald saw David run away but didn't attempt to stop him.

When a couple turned to go after David, Gerald said, "Leave the boy alone. Maybe he's got the right idea about how to handle this—just run away from it."

Gerald looked back down. He sat apart from most of the family. He wasn't crying; he was angry. His mind whirled with thoughts. Why couldn't that silly woman have done what he'd told her to do for once? He'd told her exactly what would happen. But, no, she didn't listen. And, as usual, he had been right. He was always right.

Now that she'd defied him, what was he going to do? Here he was, stuck with a funeral he couldn't afford, and with two young boys and no mother to take care of them. What a mess!

How could she have done this to him? More to the point, how could God ruin his life ... yet again?

He had to come up with a solution to fix this. And then he had an idea.

TWO

N THE DAYS following the funeral, David felt a tenseness in the air. He watched quietly, knowing something was about to happen: a change he wouldn't like and would have no control over.

David didn't have to wait long to find out what it was. The answer came when his father put two suitcases containing David's clothes in the car and then told him, "Come on, let's go."

When David didn't move, his father jerked open the car door. "Get in. I'm not going to tell you again."

David got into the car, hugging his beloved Ginger to his chest. His father's face was impassive as he fumbled for his keys and then started the car.

"Daddy," David dared to ask, "why am I going to Grandmother and Grandfather Hyler's house?"

"Because I can't take care of you," his father said swiftly.

"How long will I be there?"

Gerald ignored the question and backed out of the drive.

When his father was heading down the street and David realized there would be no answer, he asked, "What about Will?"

"That's different," his father said bluntly. "He's older. He can take care of himself."

"But ... but ... what about G'anny? Why can't I stay with her?"

"She can't take care of you."

"Why?"

His father frowned. "It doesn't matter. Stop asking silly questions."

"Why can't I stay with you?"

Gerald's face remained stoic as he said, "You just can't."

David shrank against the door, huddling with his repaired stuffed animal. He didn't understand. He would never understand.

The drive took hours, and they were hours of complete silence. David had never felt so alone, so abandoned.

The sign on the lawn said it was a children's home. Gerald turned into the drive, halted, and shouted at a worker raking the yard nearby, "You there, where's the superintendent?"

The man stopped raking and pointed. "The judge is around back."

Without a word, Gerald continued down the drive. As he rounded the corner of the house, two people came out to meet him.

Judge William Hyler was a pleasant-looking man with a bit of a spare tire around his middle but far short of being fat. He wore a three-piece blue suit, and wire-rimmed glasses were perched on his nose.

His wife, Margaret, was slender, with unnatural jet-black hair pulled back in a very severe hairstyle. She wore black-framed glasses, and her pinched expression could not be called welcoming.

The judge walked up to the car. "How was your trip, son?"

"Five hours. How do you think it was?" Gerald snapped. He removed two small suitcases from the trunk, dropped them heavily on the lawn, and then yanked opened the passenger door.

"Come on, get out," he said to David

"I don't want to stay here," David said.

Gerald jerked the stuffed animal out of David's hands. "What did you bring this for? You're too old for something like this."

He tossed it in the back of the car as David's face contorted. Gerald pointed a finger at him. "You'd better not start crying, or you'll wish you hadn't."

David grabbed him around the waist and held on tightly.

"Go over to your grandmother," Gerald insisted.

As the older couple approached, David moved behind Gerald, still clinging to his legs.

"Stop that! What's the matter with you? Let go of me and get in the house. Now!"

David clung even harder, burying his face in Gerald's leg.

"David, get in the house ... now."

An instant later, Margaret pried David loose from Gerald's leg. "Let go of your father and come with me," she ordered.

David started crying as she pulled him away.

"Stop that crying! You sound like a baby," she hissed.

Tucking one of his bags under her arm, she took the other with the same hand, keeping the other hand and arm free to drag David to the house.

David looked over his shoulder at Gerald, sniffling.

The two men continued to stand by the car.

The judge, arms clasped behind his back, walked closer to Gerald. "Son, what you're doing isn't right. David shouldn't be put in this orphanage."

Gerald glowered. "Don't lecture me, Dad. Besides, I'm not putting him in the orphanage. I'm bringing him to live with you. After all, you run this place, so what's one more kid running around?"

His father shook his head sadly. "That's not the point, and you know it. You have a responsibility to raise your sons ... both of them."

Gerald glared at him. "Just because you're a judge doesn't mean you can judge me."

"Son, there's only one Judge."

"*Hmmph.* That's according to you."

"Your son needs his father."

"He needs his mother too, but she isn't here, is she? What does your so-called Judge say about that?"

The judge put his hand on his son's shoulder, but Gerald shrugged it off. "Son, I know you're hurting ... that you feel alone and unloved."

Gerald focused an intense, challenging gaze on his father. "You have no idea what I feel. You never did. Are you going to look after David or not?"

William sighed deeply. "You know I will. I'll care for him as if he were my own son."

Gerald swiveled away, dismissing his father. "Great. I hope you do a better job with him than you did with me. He's all yours."

Spinning on his heel, Gerald got back into the driver's seat.

William reached in through the open window and retrieved Ginger. "Your son needs to keep some of his childhood."

Inside the house, his grandmother set down the bags and gave David a cursory tour of the house. "This is the dining room; this is where we eat. It is the only room you will be eating in." She bent over until she was right in his face. "Do you understand me?"

David gave a barely perceptible nod. It didn't smell like a home. He wrinkled his nose. It smelled like a hospital or doctor's office; a strong smell like the stuff that his mom used to pour out of a bottle and onto his scrapes. The thought of his mom made him sad.

They walked through an archway into a room with flowered wallpaper. It looked nice, at first. Then, he noticed the furniture. It was all very rigid with odd-looking wooden legs that had carvings in them. None of it looked comfortable—there wasn't even a pillow on any piece of furniture—and then he saw it was all covered with plastic. Everything seemed to be perfectly positioned; nothing was out of place. "This is the living room. You are not allowed in the living room ... ever."

David said the only thing he could: "Yes, ma'am." Truth be told, he didn't want to go in there anyway.

Continuing the tour, they went up the narrow stairs into a dark hallway lit only by a window on the end. He blinked his eyes, trying to adjust to the dark. They stopped in front of the first door on the left. It was open.

"This is the bathroom," she said. Then, leaning down and speaking slowly and distinctly, she added, "Don't mess it up. I will not tolerate toothpaste in the sink." Her finger in his face served to punctuate the words with added intensity and emphasis. Standing upright then turning to walk away, she continued down the hallway, saying over her shoulder, "Follow me."

The next stop was a small bedroom. "This is where you will stay."

With those words, she left him surrounded by a lonely silence.

David could only stand there, looking around the room. It was cold ... sterile ... empty. Devoid of presence and personality. Just a bed, an empty dresser, and blinds with no curtain. Not even a rug on the hard wooden floor. The room seemed as empty as his life felt to him right now.

The familiar sound of his father's car distracted David. He ran to the window and watched his father drive away, continuing to gaze plaintively in that direction even after he lost sight of him.

Without warning, the silence was broken by the sound of his grandmother's voice, cold and dripping with disdain, as she retreated back down the hallway. "I hope you're happy. You've just ruined my retirement." The click of her heavy steps on the hardwood floors punctuated her sentences.

When the footsteps faded, he was left with only an eerie, lonely silence. Again.

David took a small box from his suitcase. It had once held assorted candy in little brown wrappers, a rare gesture of affection from his father to his mother. It now held the treasured remains of his young life. It had a bronzed baby shoe and an empty bottle of his mom's favorite perfume. There was a small framed picture of him and his mother, along with a few snapshots. But his treasure was the picture he had drawn of himself and his mom that day on the porch at G'anny's house.

Nevertheless, these treasures were not comforting. They didn't make him feel better. His whole life ... in one small box.

David walked to the bed, as if he were in a trance. He climbed up on it and assumed the fetal position, drawing his legs as close to his chest as he could. Tears flowed freely. Again.

This time, no one was there to see.

Not his mother. Not his grandmother. No one.

He was alone.

Later that evening, David was again in bed, but this time dressed in his pajamas. He was lying there, staring at the ceiling in the dark room. Suddenly, he was washed in a faint light as the door opened.

His grandfather stood in the doorway, silhouetted by the light in the hallway. "David, are you all right?" he asked kindly.

"Yes, sir." David whispered.

"Did you like dinner?"

"Yes, sir."

"Did you brush your teeth?"

"Yes, sir."

"Did you say your prayers?"

"No, sir."

His grandfather moved to the side of the bed, removing his wire-rimmed glasses. "Well, why don't we do that now?"

Taking David's small hands in his, William said a simple prayer: "Now I lay me down to sleep, I pray the Lord my soul to keep. If I should die before I wake, I pray the Lord my soul to take. Amen."

His grandfather looked down at him. "Is there someone you want me to pray for? Your dad? Your brother?"

"Can we pray for my mommy?"

Grandfather's mouth toyed with a smile at the corners. "Your mommy is with Jesus now, so we don't need to pray for her. She's in a wonderful place."

But when David frowned, his grandfather smiled and then relented. "But I guess we can always use prayer, even if we are in heaven. Why don't you say it?"

David's frown changed to a smile. He bowed his head and added, "And God, please bless Daddy and Will and Mommy. And help Mommy to not be so sad from missing me, and help me to not be so sad from missing her. Amen."

His grandfather tousled David's hair. "That's a very good prayer." He stood and tucked the cover up around the small boy. "You sleep tight now."

He was almost at the door when he stopped and turned to look at David. His grandfather's eyes glimmered with kindness. "I just remembered. I have someone here who misses you." He stepped out briefly and came back with a hint of mischief on his face and something behind his back. As he returned to the side of the bed, he held out Ginger, smiling gently.

David broke out in a big grin and embraced his cherished stuffed dog.

His grandfather savored the moment and then turned to walk toward the door. At the door, he paused again. "How about if I leave this door open just a little bit? Would that be okay?"

"Yes, sir." David was relieved to not be so alone.

"Good night, son. If you need anything, you come get me, all right?"

"Yes, sir."

His grandfather smiled and then added, "I love you, David."

As promised, his grandfather left the door open a crack. David hugged Ginger to his chest and began to realize that maybe he wasn't alone after all.

Margaret met William at the foot of the stairs, arms folded across her chest. She was drawn up into a tight, compact package. Her stance by itself issued a challenge, one he'd seen many times before and ignored. He crossed the room into the kitchen to retrieve a piece of pie. He returned to the room to find Margaret as stoic as ever.

"William," she stated as he sat down at the table.

The judge sat at the table, held up his hand to her, and then bowed his head to say grace over the small snack he had brought with him, continuing to ignore what he knew to be coming.

But she would not be put off. As soon as he finished with the prayer, she said a bit too loudly, "We've raised our son. We've done our part. It's time for us to be able to enjoy the rest of our lives."

The judge put a finger to his lips. "*Shh!* He'll hear you."

"So what? I don't care if he does. And don't you shush me."

Frustrated, he got up, took her by the arm, and led her into the kitchen. In a quiet yet firm voice, he tried to reason with her. "Margaret, how can we enjoy life when our grandson has been orphaned? God is very clear on how we are supposed to take care of widows and orphans."

She jerked her arm away from where he had his hand on her elbow. "Don't you preach to me, William Hyler. Save that for somebody who cares. He isn't an orphan; he has a father. How could you saddle us with such a burden at this time in our lives?"

He stared in disbelief at his wife. After all these years, he still could not understand how she could be so self-centered and angry. He held his hands up in a gesture of supplication, then let them fall. "A father? Our son has chosen this path, and David needs us. What would you have me do? Turn him out into the street?"

She looked at him as if he were mentally impaired. "Don't you get it? He's not supposed to be our problem."

The judge turned his eyes to the ceiling, or perhaps beyond it. "He's not a problem; he's a child. Our grandchild!"

Margaret stomped off. "I don't want to talk about it anymore. I'm going to bed!" she retorted angrily. "But this isn't over. Not by a long shot."

"No, I know it isn't over," the judge muttered to himself. "Nothing is ever over with you, Margaret."

Meanwhile, upstairs and alone in his room, David listened to the argument. He seemed to be constantly lying in the dark, listening to someone argue about him. First at his home. And now in this place.

David listened as his grandmother went to her room, slamming the door behind her. Shortly afterward, he heard another door close, softly this time. He then heard a curious swishing sound, and he went to the window.

Below, illuminated by the streetlight, he saw his grandfather sweeping the sidewalk with slow, gentle strokes.

THREE

T HE DAYS PASSED slowly for David in his new home. Days became weeks. Weeks became months. And none of them were peaceful. But he had found that his grandpa was a calm at the center of what seemed to be a constant storm. He came to realize that his grandpa was someone he could trust. David needed that. He also needed to understand what was going on.

"Grandpa," David asked, "can I ask you something?"

William smiled and put his hand on David's shoulder. "Of course. You can ask me anything."

"Why am I living here instead of with G'anny?"

William's shoulders shook with a silent laugh. He knew, given a choice of grandmothers, what David's choice would be. And he couldn't blame the boy. "I think you are entitled to understand that. Let's sit over here on the porch." They settled beside each other on a bench.

"It's a little complicated," William began.

"What does that mean?"

"It's a word that means there isn't just a simple answer."

"Oh."

William studied his grandson's face as he explained the situation. "I know you were close with your other grandmother and really would have liked to live there. But, you see, she's in poor health. She could look after you for short stretches but simply isn't strong enough to take you in on a full-time basis. I know she loves you very much and would give anything to be able to do it, but she just isn't able. Do you understand that?"

"I think so."

"Good. Because she loves you very much and I want to make sure you know it isn't that she didn't want to."

SPRING 1975

After four years of living in this house, David learned that he could never please his grandmother—no matter what he did or did not do, and no matter how hard he tried. He learned the best thing he could do was try to spend as much time in his room as possible.

But his relationship with his grandfather was far different. Grandpa, as David called him, was gentle and kind, sort of like his mom. He was also strong and confident, even though he was under an almost constant attack from his wife. David didn't understand where that strength came from—but it was something he knew he need in his life as well.

That afternoon, David approached the handyman taking a break from the yard work in the shade of one of the large pecan trees. The man had always been friendly to him, but David knew him only as Jack.

"How ya doing, David?"

"I'm okay," David said, then sat beside Jack.

Out of the corner of his eye, he saw his grandfather sweeping the walk again.

Jack nodded toward the walk. "Guess your grandpa has run afoul of the missus again. Ain't right that he has to put up with all that caterwauling. He's a good man. Deserves better, I say."

"I think so too."

Jack studied David, then relaxed, as if he'd made up his mind about something that needed to be said. "You know, he ain't the type to blow his own horn, and I know that woman of his ain't bragged on him any to you. Betcha don't know how much your grandpa has done for folks around here."

David shook his head. "He doesn't talk about himself very much."

"Didn't figure he had. Take this orphanage, for instance. He took this place over back in 1933, when it was in the red—so much that it didn't even make sense to foreclose on it. You see, it was sponsored by a fraternal organization, and they had orphanages all over the country. The judge surprised everybody by not only turning the finances around but also having a capital fund drive. He started building dormitories and other buildings so successfully that by the time they were opened up, they were paid for. No small feat considering we was in the middle of the Great Depression."

"Are you serious? He did that?"

"This place is on 144 acres of land, and you can see the judge has managed to turn it into a working farm. He was so good at it that it helped to feed people in town during World War II, when food started becoming scarce. And when the local pastor went off to war, your grandpa served as the pastor of the church in town. Sometimes he held services right here on the grounds of the orphanage."

"I've never heard that either."

"I figured as much. Betcha you don't know how he come to be the judge either."

"No."

"That's quite a story in itself. Back in the early '60s they wanted him to run for the position of judge, but he wouldn't do it. But people wouldn't take no for an answer. After the election, the newspaper called to ask him what he thought about being elected, and that was the first he knew of it. He'd won it in a landslide, and he did it by write-in votes. The people who actually ran for the office only got eleven votes between 'em."

"Wow."

"Kept getting elected the same way. That's quite a thing. He never did actually run for office." Jack grinned.

David grinned back. "That sounds like him."

"Funny how he's so strong in everything he does, but that woman he's matched up to just runs over him like he was nothing."

"When I came here, they had already told the people they were going to retire. That was eight year ago."

"Yep, the organization was having money problems and was looking to kinda consolidate things. Reckon it seemed to make sense to consolidate closer to big cities, since this home is in such small town. Besides, like you said, the judge and his wife were planning to retire anyway, so they decided this would be one that was closed. Not immediately, of course. Before orphans were placed somewhere else, they tried to find family members who might take them. That took time."

David looked down at the ground a said quietly, "Yeah, I know."

Jack gave David a knowing look. "I guess you would know that one. I reckon that kinda left you in a sort of no-man's land, didn't it? I've seen how the kids at the orphanage haven't had nothing to do with you, on account of how you live with the superintendent. And I've seen how you ain't welcomed by your grandmother either."

Jack paused as David continued to study the dirt. In a moment of silence that suddenly became awkward, David looked up at Jack.

Jack looked right a David to emphasize his next statement. "And I've also seen how your grandpa cares for you. You might not realize it and all, but he loves you."

Jack let that sink it before continuing. As David turned to look at his grandfather in the distance, Jack continued. "Well, I reckon they've about got all the kids placed now, so it won't be long before they close this place."

David turned back to Jack. Genuinely concerned, he asked, "Will you lose your job?"

"I imagine so. But reckon I'm due to retire too. I'll probably just do yard work on the side. That way, I can do as much as I want to do without nobody to tell me to come or git." He got to his feet. "Well, I've enjoyed this little talk, but I gotta get back to work while I still have a job."

"Thanks for telling me all this."

Jack nodded. "I figured you deserved to know about your grandpa, and I knew he wasn't the kind of man to tell you. Like I said, I knew that old harpy wasn't going to do it." He wrinkled his nose, making his perceptions clear. "Just seeing him under her thumb he might not look to you to stand too tall, but in this community, he casts a really long shadow."

As the orphanage edged toward closing, one by one, kids were placed either in other orphanages elsewhere in the country or, in some cases, with distant family members. Slowly, life came to halt and the once-vibrant hub of a community began to resemble that of a ghost town. More than five hundred lives had been impacted, and now, only one was left with a very uncertain future.

As the new year rolled around, David and his grandparents moved into town when the orphanage formally closed. Even though David was only nine, he knew in his heart that, if it had been up to his grandmother, he would have been placed somewhere too. He now found himself trapped in close proximity to his grandparents, and his grandfather no longer had the running of the orphanage to occupy his time.

With the new year came a new school. What wasn't new was that David had trouble making any friends. In part, this might have been because of the front he put up to protect himself. It was a false bravado that most could not penetrate; nor did they want to try. Truth be told, he didn't want them to. Being alone had begun to feel like a safe place.

David still missed the life he thought he was supposed to have—a life others seemed to enjoy but that he was denied. He especially missed his mother. Why did God have to take her from him? It was a question that was never far from his mind. It was a question that continually fueled a growing anger and sense of frustration. And then there was his father.

FOUR

SUNDAY, AUGUST 1976

D AVID AGAIN HEARD his grandfather sweeping the walk just as he'd done so many times at the orphanage. He stepped over to watch him from the window of his bedroom.

A door slammed, and Margaret walked up to his grandfather. They were obviously continuing an argument David hadn't heard, but now her words were loud enough that he couldn't miss them.

"Don't you walk away from me when I'm talking to you," she challenged. "You can't hide behind that broom forever."

The teenager shook his head. *Here we go again,* he said to himself. *Why does Grandpa put up with that?*

David left the window and sat on the edge of his bed. He reached into the nightstand and pulled out his familiar box of mementos, opening it gently.

The argument continued outside, but the words were indistinct now. The sound of sweeping had stopped. David pulled his treasured picture from the box: a folded crayon drawing of a little boy holding his mommy's hand. He remembered when he'd made that drawing—the day his world had come crashing down. He remembered G'anny and how nice she always was to him ... a far cry from the shrew yelling at his grandfather out front. He couldn't even think of that woman in the same terms as his other grandmother—only as "Margaret," because she seemed to want no family connection at all to him.

Margaret apparently had the last word and slammed the front door as she went back into the house. He shook his head again. She slammed doors a lot. It was a wonder half the hinges in the house weren't broken. Or maybe his grandfather just quietly fixed them—the way he quietly fixed everything.

He heard the swishing of the broom again. They had to have the cleanest sidewalk in the entire county. He replaced the memento box and picked up a worn book from the nightstand. It was a dog-eared Bible. He started to open it but hesitated. Something else was calling him. He gently placed the Bible back on his nightstand, got up, and went out to talk to his grandfather.

"Grandpa, why do you let her talk to you like that?" he said as he came up behind the older man where he stood sweeping the walk.

His grandfather smiled, seemingly unaffected by the tongue-lashing David had just heard. Even after all these years, David didn't understand how his grandfather could stay so calm.

The older man stopped sweeping. "Talk to me how, son?"

David shrugged. "You know ... ugly, disrespectful."

Grandpa smiled gently again and returned to his sweeping. David moved around in front of him. "Remember what Jesus said, son: 'No man is without honor except in his own house.'"

David frowned. "But aren't you angry? When she talks to you like that, doesn't it make you want to break something?"

His grandfather chuckled. "I'd just have to fix it."

"Why don't you divorce her?" David blurted.

Grandpa stopped sweeping again and looked off into the distance. "Well, son, by the laws of man I suppose I could, based on the grounds of incompatibility. But by the laws of God, I can't." He went back to sweeping again.

David watched for a few moments. "At least tell me why you are always sweeping. I've seen you do it for years now."

"Because it accomplishes something good, and anger doesn't. Solomon said—"

David sighed. "Solomon again? You're always quoting Solomon."

"Why do you think that is?" His grandfather was always in teaching mode. He didn't just lecture or give orders. He took time to help David understand.

"I don't know. I just know you do it a lot."

"It's because God uses the book of Proverbs to compare the lifestyles of those willing to serve and those who are merely living for themselves. Proverbs makes a strong case for living by God's design and not our own. At the heart of God's design is the basic idea that we must accept His love. One of the ways we do that is by moving forward and not dwelling in the past."

"I get it. You sweep as a way of accomplishing something good and not dwelling in the past or on the argument."

"Very good, son." David liked it when his grandfather called him that. He always did it with genuine affection and a slight smile.

His grandfather continued. "It's my way of moving forward and preparing myself for the next opportunity from God. For example, I think it's Proverbs 21 that says, 'The horse is prepared for the day of battle, but the victory belongs to the Lord.'"

"I don't get that."

"It means all of our preparations for any task are useless without God, but even with God's help we must still do our part and prepare. His control of the outcome does not negate our responsibilities. God will use us if we are well prepared. If we dwell in the past and hang on to the hurt, we can't be prepared for the victories he has in store for us."

David nodded slowly. "I see."

"Do you? The principles of the Bible are not just abstract things intended for somebody else. We don't really 'see' until we see how they apply in our own lives."

"What do you mean?"

"David, God has something in store for you. He'll use you if you're well prepared. But you have to learn to let go of the hurt in your past so you can be prepared for the victories He's planned for you in the future." Grandfather returned to his sweeping.

David went back into the house, only to emerge moments later with another broom. He ran to his grandfather's side. Smiling, David began to sweep in unison with his grandfather.

FIVE

JULY 1980

D AVID HAD JUST turned eighteen when things began to come to a head. He still had no contact with the father who had kicked him out, and now Margaret had done the same—sent him away. In the process and in typical fashion, she steamrolled over the top of his grandfather. At first glance, one might easily have concluded that decades of her attitude had worn the man down. But such was not the case. Instead, he went along with it, believing it to be in the boy's best interest to be away from the woman. It was an option he couldn't take for himself, but at least David could be free. And he knew David was ready to fly ... whether David believed it or not.

Creativity was one thing David did not lack. He especially enjoyed photography and art. Pursuing these interests led him to his first job, with an architectural arts firm, which, as fate would have it, also had an apartment for rent upstairs over the office. It was a small, one-room apartment, but it met his needs and was affordable. He finally had a place he could call his own.

But it provided no comfort from the feelings that continued to haunt David. He was again feeling very alone and abandoned, as what had passed for a home had been taken from him. Yet, in spite of his grandfather going along with him moving out, he knew this man was the one person who never lost faith in him. When he would sit alone thinking, some of the gentle words would come to him in the judge's voice: "God made you for a reason. God made you very special. God gave you a life, the greatest gift He could give you. The best thing you can do is to do something with it."

He had always gone to church—first his mother, and then his grandfather had seen to that. But he felt like he'd been living with a "borrowed" religion. He'd absorbed only head knowledge, not heart knowledge. Now, through understanding, he began developing a faith of his own.

Over time, David began to realize his grandfather was speaking to him of his spiritual life. His grandfather had always taught him in parables, examples, and suddenly the blinders came off. The truth of the judge's words was blindingly clear. God had accepted him as His child. David was a child of the King! Now all David had to do was accept this truth.

Even with a developing faith, David still had no direction in his life. Wandering aimlessly wasn't a future. His job was just that—a job. It paid the bills but didn't seem to have a future. He needed something with purpose, with structure, and with a future. It was at this point that the logical next step, to David, seemed to be the military. Everyone said the army took boys and turned them into men. With only his grandfather to guide him in his own transition to manhood, that saying made sense to David.

The thought of basic training wasn't all that appealing. Still. He knew it was going to be hard, but he also knew it was going to be good for him. Besides, when he finished his enlistment, they would pay for his college. David thought he was prepared.

But how did someone prepare for Sergeant First Class Jackson? The instant the group of recruits arrived, Drill Sergeant Jackson began screaming at them to get them off the bus, lining them up in ranks, going to first one and then the other, yelling mere inches from their faces. David stood there in shock, thinking, *What have I done?*

The objective of a drill sergeant is to train soldiers to obey orders without wasting a lot of time questioning why. Drill sergeants are very good at this, and the first day is critical, getting the "boots" into a condition of shock from the very beginning. Jackson came down on one recruit after another, in no particular order, heaping what seemed like abuse on them. But this was nothing new to David. And while the army would not use the word *abuse,* preferring instead the term *discipline,* he knew what it felt like to him.

The next stop for the recruits was standing in line at the supply depot to draw uniforms, rifles, and gear.

The recruit next to David looked over at him in admiration. "Man, he really came down on you, and it rolled off you like water off a duck. I think that made him even madder. How did you handle that so well?"

David smiled a small smile. "Trust me, Sergeant Jackson is an amateur compared to my grandmother. I've been trained for this."

The soldier gave him a confused look. If he only knew.

David hadn't thought about this aspect of training. Ironic that he was trying to escape a life of abuse, only to walk head-on into the place that had taken confrontation to a fine art. But this was the purpose of basic training—calculated mental conditioning, coupled with short nights and intense physical regimens. It had probably been used since the time of Old Testament armies and had proved to produce well-trained, well-disciplined soldiers. It was also six weeks of pure hell.

Infractions produced demands for an unreasonable number of push-ups or pull-ups. Hikes tested the limits of endurance, coupled with obstacle courses to quickly take them beyond what they would have thought they could do. The objective was for each man to find his point of endurance so that he could build it from there.

They fell into bed exhausted, able to be asleep literally within a minute or less. They were rushed through three big meals a day, forced to wolf them down in minutes before getting back into action. They would find themselves out doing PT before the sun was even up: jumping jacks in unison, push-ups until their arms ached, and marching, always marching, everywhere they would go.

Then came the gas chamber. They marched single file into the concrete building, gas masks securely in place. One by one, they were required to remove them, give their name, rank, and serial number, and answer a few questions asked by a sergeant who, remarkably, was standing there with no mask on at all through the whole process. The trainees would then run outside to gag and cough from the tear gas.

Next, followed hours on the rifle ranges and the grenade range, and David's personal favorite: crawling in mud under a barbed-wire obstacle course while live machine-gun rounds sang overhead. Simulated artillery rounds exploded practically in his ear, and the acrid stench of gunpowder permeated his clothing to the point where he reeked of it constantly. And they hiked out to each exercise, always marching, marching.

Even through this turmoil, David's past served him well. Perhaps he coped because of it. Either way, he was able to focus better than most in the midst of the noise and misery, earning his expert marksmanship ribbon for both the M-16 rifle and the 9-mm handgun.

The recruits became machines, too tired to think, simply reacting to orders. And the days dragged on until they thought basic would never end.

But it did.

David found himself standing in ranks at the graduation ceremony as his basic training unit had successfully completed training. The unit would now be broken up as people went to a variety of assignments in the real army. The men were now conditioned to obey orders, and that would continue through their days of service. However, unlike other times in his life, the abuse was over. David hoped his life was changing for the better and that the ceremony he was part of was marking that change.

Life after training was different. For the first time in his life, David found himself able to earn respect based on his accomplishments. If he hustled, applied himself, and focused on serving others, he found he could earn promotions and awards. It was that last part, serving others, that began to truly resonate with him. It was a fundamental premise of his faith in Christ. And the military—unknowingly, he was sure—became a great place to refine the skills of his faith. In so doing, the lessons from his grandfather began to take on greater meaning and importance. He soon realized he'd become who he was because of the patient and gentle love of his grandfather. So, it seemed only fitting that upon being recognized for his first award, a very special commendation medal, he gave it to his grandfather. In David's mind, it really belonged to him.

This was the first of many awards. David applied himself so strongly with a heart of service that he was selected for Officer Candidate School, where he continued to excel, finishing at the top of his class. But before he could be an officer, David had to have a college degree, which involved an assignment to college, with a return to active duty upon graduation. The army had promised to turn him into a man, and they had. They also succeeded in turning him into a leader.

As a boy who had always been totally subject to the will of others, David now reveled in a new feeling of control over his own destiny.

JULY 1982

The army surprised David when they told him the choice of a college was up to him. David hadn't expected that kind of freedom! But after a lot of deliberation between large versus small schools, secular versus faith, he decided to visit a small, private Southern Baptist university in North Carolina. He'd heard of the school while he has in high school, mainly from people in his church. After his first visit, he knew this was the place he needed to be. It felt safe compared to large universities. Here, he was a name, not a number. Consequently, they treated him as a person—as someone who had potential. It was a newfound sense of respect and worth, unlike any he'd sensed before, except from his grandfather. Ultimately, he chose this school because the people made him feel special—as if he mattered.

As he walked onto the campus, he was immediately struck by the difference in feel from the army posts he'd been on. It was a lovely campus, reflective of the Deep South and of antebellum days gone by. It was like taking a step back in time. *A time "gone with the wind,"* he thought, smiling as it occurred to him. It did bring the old movie to mind.

Trees and beautifully manicured lawns were abundant. And the buildings. What was it about the buildings? He chuckled. They just looked smart, as though they were full of knowledge and had been for many years.

On his foray around campus, a girl gave him a quick smile.

"Miss? Excuse me," he dared to say. "I'm looking for registration."

She pointed. "That's the administration building, and the registrar's office is on the second floor."

"Thank you."

As he headed toward the building, time seemed to freeze. He felt like he was imprinting this scene on his memory for all time. This was the first day of the rest of his life—he could feel it. He'd had that feeling when he got into the army, but now he knew that was just preparation, grooming, to prepare him for what had to come now. This was it.

Even when he was registered, installed in the dorm, this new experience still didn't seem real. Never before had he been greeted so warmly and welcomed so openly by so many total strangers.

But it got real. Walking back to the student union, he met two guys in football jerseys. They stopped in front of him. He looked at them quizzically.

"Give way, fish."

"Fish?"

The taller boy smirked. The forty-four on his jersey marked him as a lineman. His companion, a linebacker, wore fifty-two. "Boy, *fish* are what we call freshmen. When fish see upperclassmen coming, they get off the sidewalk."

David sighed. He hadn't counted on being a freshman, on starting over.

"And where's your beanie, boy? Freshmen have to wear that beanie. You trying to make people think you aren't a fish?"

Fifty-two said, "Don't let us catch you without that beanie again, or we'll make you sorry."

"Yeah, and we'll be looking for you."

David gave way, and they swaggered past and on down the sidewalk.

The euphoria left him. He was starting over again, all right.

A short while later, David was one of a dozen freshmen sitting around the lobby of the dorm, discussing their new surroundings.

"Hazing is nothing new," one boy said. "My old man told me about how it was in his day. He pledged a fraternity, and he said it really got rough there."

"I read where it goes all the way back to Plato's Academy," David added. "That's two thousand years ago."

The other boys turned to him in shock. "Are you kidding me, geek? Is there anything you won't read?"

He shrugged. "Not much."

"I just know that sometimes it gets out of hand," another boy said. "I read in the paper the other day that two boys died because of a binge-drinking thing that was part of pledging on another campus near here."

"That's stupid," David said, but he also understood the lengths people would go to in order to find acceptance.

The first boy stared at him. "I saw those football players get in your face. It didn't seem to faze you."

David grinned. "Once you've had a drill sergeant with garlic breath screaming an inch away from your nose at four in the morning, those guys are strictly amateur."

"Ex-military, huh?"

"Not ex."

"You see any action?"

"Some."

"Wow, what was that like?"

"I learned two rules of life. Rule number one: Young men die. Rule number two: Nobody can change rule number one. So, if you don't mind, I'd really rather not talk about it."

"I get it. That's cool with me."

It only took a month or two for the beanies to start disappearing; the upperclassmen got bored with it, and everyone turned to the task of getting an education. Either that, or they seemed determined to party until they could no longer manage to stay in school. David had no intention of wasting his opportunity.

He wasn't that much older than the kids coming in straight from high school, but his maturity level after his military experience made him seem much older. With his military background, he automatically stepped up to assume leadership in any class he was in.

His time in the service gave him an interest in computers as well as some practical experience. His math major also caused him to gravitate into computer science, with more emphasis on software development than on hardware. He turned out to have a gift for it and excelled in his classes.

On the surface, David had grown and matured, but many of the scars of his youth remained just below the surface, cropping up at some of the most unexpected times. In his studies and in his continuing role in the army reserves, he was the strong and confident leader. In the solitude of his personal time, he was still plagued by lingering insecurities.

David's degree was in math. Not because he had a great love for the subject—that came later, during his course of study. Rather, his love was engineering, because he enjoyed building things and figuring out how they worked. But he chose math because he was driven not to just move past a failure but to completely and thoroughly overcome it. Some would suggest this was more of an obsession than a simple character trait.

His issue with math had arisen years earlier. During his first semester in math in the eighth grade, his teachers selected him for an advanced class that introduced him to algebra a year early. Excited, honored, and a little overwhelmed, he accepted the challenge. He failed, rather miserably and spectacularly. Though his teachers were patient and encouraging, his grandmother made sure he knew how much of a disappointment and complete failure he was. *Nothing new there,* he thought.

It was not for her, but for the teachers who stood with him and helped him, that he worked hard and bore down on the subject. At that point, math became something in which he could excel. It wasn't something he enjoyed, but, in his mind, it was his way of apologizing to and thanking his teachers, while at the same time proving his grandmother wrong. And it opened the door to many other subjects he loved, such as physics and other sciences. So, in the end, earning a degree in the subject that had taunted him early on seemed only natural.

Years later, with the tools needed to understand other sciences, he would go on to study what he truly enjoyed. In so doing, he earned his master's and doctoral degrees, both in engineering. And both with numerous academic honors that, in his mind, would prove his grandmother wrong once and for all. He was not a failure. At least in no one's eyes but hers. But all this was yet to come. In the present, David graduated from college with his undergraduate degree and received his commission. Full speed ahead.

Not long after, David was dealt another blow as his grandfather was taken by cancer. In spite of a strengthening faith base, and even though David had been making himself something of a home in the military, he again found himself beset with that familiar feeling of being alone in the world. But this time, he had the sage counsel of his grandfather to comfort him. Though difficult to see amid the grief of loss, these cherished memories would serve him well in the coming years.

SIX

JUNE 1994

D AVID KNEW WHAT it felt like to be berated, having experienced that for much of his life, and had no intention of doing that to others. His grandfather had shown him a better way. It was a way that made David a caring and compassionate officer, sensitive to the needs of those placed under him. As a new second lieutenant, David threw himself into his assignments, often finding himself doing things normally reserved for more-senior officers. When he was promoted to first lieutenant, he was immediately placed in a position where he supervised more than 350 people—a position he found out had traditionally been filled by a higher rank. A compulsive overachiever, David tried to compensate for a lack of achievement early in life. He was trying to fill a void in his life that he couldn't put a name to. For now, he called it work. When he made captain, that work took him to the Pentagon.

Unlike so many things in his life over which he had no control, once he learned how things worked in the military, he got very good at it. Stepping up and stepping out became routine for him. So, it came as no surprise to anyone that he would volunteer (and be chosen) for a selectively manned position at US Central Command during the Gulf War. As with each of his previous assignments, this one thrust him into a world unlike any he'd experienced. But this time, he learned it was to be unlike anything he could have imagined. He learned quickly that training for war was one thing; living one was quite another.

The battle staff at USCENTCOM was as different from the Pentagon as night was from day. But his drive and determination to excel took over. During the next four years, David was involved in every real-world operation in the Middle East and northeast Africa. Promoted ahead of his peers, at the age of twenty-eight, he became the youngest major in his branch of the service. Now sporting the gold oak leaves of a major, he also earned a number of awards. His future was brighter than he'd dreamed possible. That is, until the famous incident in Somalia that became known as Black Hawk Down.

Many of the US operations he'd been involved with had been successful. But David couldn't get the failure of Somalia out of his mind. He knew failure was a part of any operation. It was also a means for growth and learning. But losing friends in a land that already seemed so lost itself was too much. Watching them die was one thing ... and hard enough to handle. Looking into the eyes of the starving, hopeless children left behind in that ravaged landscape was another. He hadn't been prepared. The scars of his past—his own fear and abandonment—were ripped open, and the tears flowed. Again. No number of awards, or promotions, would stem the tide. Once again, he felt helpless to impact those around him. The old uncertainty washed over David like a tsunami. He'd been thinking about making the military a career. Now it seemed to be last place on earth he wanted to be.

AUGUST 1996

David left active duty. He still felt the need to serve, just not as he'd been doing. He'd worked hard for his commission, so, rather than surrender it, David transferred into the reserves and began pursuing civilian opportunities.

It was then that the first angel entered David's life.

SEVEN

T'S ONE OF the curious paradoxes in life that time often passes far too slowly. Kids think it takes forever for summer to roll around. It may be only a week before your birthday, yet it seems it will never arrive. And waiting for Christmas to get here? Well, that goes without saying. While waiting for something in the future, time can pass with excruciatingly slowness. But time in the past? That's different. Reflecting back, time passes at a blinding speed.

For David, pondering his childhood, it seemed to have passed in a blur. Except the memory of a dog long ago. That one remained fixed—clearly focused and immovable.

It was time to address that issue from the past. He got a dog of his own. Whether or not it would be the special dog his mother had promised he'd have someday was something that, well, only time could tell. The dog's name was Smokey. He was a German shepherd with the classic tan-and-black coat. But his past was far from attractive. Smokey had been abused.

Literally tied to a tree for three years and wanting attention badly, he barked all the time. That is, until one day, when his owner finally had enough of it and took him to the local pound. At this point, one might think that such a handsome and regal dog would immediately get adopted, but it didn't work out that way. Fearful of break-ins because of the drugs kept at the facility, the manager of the pound tried to make Smokey a guard dog and gave him run of the facility at night.

Continued poor care and living conditions resulted in Smokey contracting heartworms. The condition went undiagnosed, so that over time he began to slow down and eventually lost his appetite. He became emaciated, and his coat lost its luster. Fights with other dogs notwithstanding, he lost his usefulness to the manager, who decided to euthanize Smokey on Christmas Eve.

It was then that a local rescue group heard about Smokey and his plight. They immediately stepped in to save him from euthanasia and began seeking medical help for his condition. At the same time, they began a huge effort to find his forever home. This time, people were interested in him—eighty-six families, to be exact, all trying to adopt him—all in line ahead of David to meet Smokey.

When David contacted the rescue, the staff set forth very clear rules and expectations.

"We want Smokey to choose his own family," the center's director told David. "Given his past of neglect and abuse, it will be important for him to decide who he'll trust and who he won't."

"I understand," said David. And he did. It was a past he could identify with.

The director went on to say, "Don't get your hopes up, Mr. Hyler. So far, he's made it clear he doesn't want to be around anyone—human or canine."

"What do you mean?" asked David.

"You're the eighty-seventh applicant. We've worked through the list of potential owners, and so far, all he's done is bark, bare his teeth, and act antisocial toward each and every one of them."

"Is he scared, or what?"

"We don't think it's fear. He's simply been beaten down so much that he doesn't seem to care one way or the other. He just wants to be left alone."

David could understand that. "I still want to meet him."

There was silence on the other end of the line. "You're the last one, Mr. Hyler. We decided to close the adoption and make him a permanent foster. We're a no-kill rescue, so he won't be put down, but he won't have a home either. So, if he reacts to you the same as all the others, that's it. Be prepared."

Prepared he was. He was ready for Smokey's reaction and knew he would need to be patient. The staff, on the other hand, wasn't. Amazement and disbelief would best describe the surprise felt by everyone when David entered the room, and they witnessed Smokey immediately coming to him, as if he were a long-lost friend. Smokey allowed David to stroke him and then promptly sat beside his new friend. Smokey had made his choice. The staff was moved and astounded. Several were even in tears, starting with the director. All of this was being ignored by Smokey—he was focused on David, who, obviously and immediately said he'd take the dog.

Perhaps Smokey recognized the need David had—for acceptance and unconditional love. For sure, David recognized the dog had the same need and was determined to meet it. The bond was immediate. But it appeared it would be short-lived.

A mere five weeks later, disaster struck.

Heartworm is a nasty disease, one that requires weeks, sometimes months, to treat. It was time for another round. Shortly after David gave Smokey his heartworm meds, Smokey began having trouble breathing and then collapsed at his feet. Realizing there was no time to lose, David rushed him to the vet, who, fortunately, was his best friend. Though that friend lived right next door, he was at his clinic.

David drove far too fast, making the normal twenty-minute trip to the clinic in under ten minutes. He pushed through the door with the sign that read "Dr. Jonathon Miller, DVM," carrying Smokey in his arms. After a quick assessment on the run, Jon called out to his staff, "He's crashing. Get a cart ready."

Without taking his eyes off Smokey, Jon began directing David to the back and had him lay Smokey on a gurney. Smokey lay practically lifeless as they worked over him. "David, go wait out front. I've got him. I'll be out in a minute."

David was frozen … nearly as unresponsive as his dog. Jon glanced at his friend, then directed one of his technicians to help. "Andrea, help David out to the lobby."

An eternity seemed to pass before Jon came out twenty minutes later.

"David, would you come with me?" Jon escorted his friend to an exam room, where there was a set of X-rays on a wall viewer. Even David could see the X-rays showed a major problem with Smokey's heart and lungs.

"David, it's not good. I've done everything I know. I've been able to get him to relax and rest a bit, but the damage the heartworms have done to his lungs is just too severe. The scar tissue and inflammation are worse than I would have ever imagined. I'm sorry to say this, but I don't think he's going to make it. I'm so sorry," Jon said, adding, "And I don't think prolonging this is in his best interest."

"He has to make it," David insisted. "He simply has to. I won't accept anything else. I just can't."

When Jon gazed at David with compassion, David knew his friend understood. He knew some of David's history. He knew that, right now, David losing Smokey from his life would be a much greater loss than just the average person losing a pet.

But David also saw the truth in his veterinarian friend's eyes. Smokey was in critical condition. And David knew enough about veterinary medicine to know Smokey would not likely survive.

"Okay, David, let's see how he does over the weekend. We'll keep him here in the hospital and closely monitored. But if he goes into respiratory distress again, you need to be prepared to let him go. Deal?"

"On one condition, Jon."

"What's that?"

"I sit with him. He needs to know I'm here for him no matter what. Understand?"

"Yes, David, I do. You can stay. You guys need each other at this point."

David sat with Smokey in his kennel all weekend, holding the dog's head in his lap. Occasionally, the animal's tail would wag—just once: up, then down … that being all the strength he had.

David recalled his grandfather's words about praying. "Pray without ceasing," he had quoted from the Good Book, as he always called it. So,

David prayed ... and prayed some more. He prayed without ceasing over a dog that had chosen him when no one else would do so.

On Sunday, David went home to clean up and go to church. Immediately after the service, he hurried back to the clinic to resume his vigil and his prayers. It was late in the evening when he finally went home to prepare for the upcoming week. Smokey was no better. But, on the other hand, he was no worse. Either way, tomorrow was going to be a long day of work—made longer by Smokey's absence and David's fears.

The next morning, before he could return to the clinic, his phone rang, and panic set in. His heart nearly stopped as he recognized Jon's voice. He steeled himself for the news. "David, you can come and get him."

"What?" David blinked in surprise.

"He's all right. He was sitting up in his kennel this morning, as if nothing had happened. I couldn't believe it, so I ran X-rays on him again. All signs of scarring are gone."

David scratched his head. "What? Is that possible?"

"No, actually it isn't possible, but I double-checked, and the scarring simply isn't there."

David paused. "But that makes no sense."

"None at all." Jon chuckled. "The staff here has nicknamed him 'the miracle puppy,' because that is sure enough what he is. And that's what happened during the night—a miracle."

While David had pushed the limits of his car to get Smokey to the hospital, he nearly flew to go pick him up to bring him home.

After that incident, Smokey never left David's side. They were inseparable. The dog would constantly insert himself between David and anyone, just in case there would be a problem, but was not aggressive and was mostly friendly to people.

Both had found what they needed in one another. And they both knew it.

EIGHT

THE BIBLE SAYS God works in mysterious ways. He also works for His people, through His people. David had learned this firsthand on more than one occasion. He also learned that while most Christians accepted this principle, they often didn't have a true understanding of what that really meant until it happened to them.

For example, David enjoyed singing in the choir at church. Also in the choir was a nodding acquaintance, a woman named Hope. It made no difference that David had no thoughts in that direction. God probably smiled gently as He started things in motion. Something He did with another one of His people.

"David?"

He turned to the sound of the familiar voice and smiled. "Hi, Sharon." Sharon was a Realtor and had taken it upon herself to make sure David found a good home and began to meet people.

"I've got someone I'd like you to meet." She guided him by the arm a few steps across the choir room to come face-to-face with Hope. "You know Hope, right?"

David extended his hand, though a bit awkwardly. "Uh, yes ... we're acquainted. How are you, Hope?"

"Very well, thank you." She politely shook the proffered hand.

All smiles, Sharon continued. "I don't know if you're aware, but Hope has a dental practice. Now, she's great dentist, but she needs a little computer help, and, if I recall, you know something about those things. I thought you might be willing to give her a hand."

"I wouldn't want to impose," Hope said quickly, trying to alleviate some of the awkwardness she felt. "But if you were able to help, I would be very grateful." Before she lost her nerve, she added, "It's a small office system that runs on our PCs."

David wondered if Hope was as nervous over this introduction as he was. Nevertheless, he smiled politely. "I'd love to be able to help, but I'm afraid I don't work on small systems, particularly PC-based ones. Most of what I do is on large mainframes for corporate businesses. I don't know anything about the medical industry, either, so I wouldn't know what would be required."

Hope nodded. "I understand."

Sharon smiled and patted David on the arm. "Well, it was worth a try."

Something told both David and Hope this wouldn't be Sharon's last attempt at trying to help.

Two weeks later, David suddenly found himself face-to-face with Hope at church. Seeking to make conversation, he resorted to the only common ground they had. "How are you today? Were you able to get your computer problem solved?"

"No, I'm afraid I haven't."

"I'm sorry to hear that. I'm sorry I can't help."

"I know. It's okay, really." Picking up her choir folder, she headed out toward the choir loft.

David felt … what? Guilty? She was obviously disappointed. *But I don't have time for another project,* he thought, *particularly one that can't possibly pay what I'm accustomed to receiving from large companies. Sure, I could probably do it, but there's just no way I can fit it in.*

A week later, they again met in the choir room. This time, the feeling of guilt struck David before they even spoke, and he realized it wasn't going to go away. Maybe he was supposed to do this. It took but a moment to find out that the computer problems still hadn't been addressed.

"I suppose I could take a look at it," he said reluctantly.

"That would be wonderful," Hope said with a hopeful tone to her voice.

"I'm making no promises," David warned.

She smiled a genuine and warm smile. "I understand."

They turned and walked toward the choir loft together.

"How would Wednesday be for you?" he asked.

"Perfect. I don't schedule patients on Wednesday afternoons, so after lunch would be great."

On Wednesday, David arrived on schedule and stood for a few minutes while Hope talked with her receptionist. Hope really was quite pretty, he noted. Tall, a trim figure, and blond hair that fell past her shoulders. *Beautiful* was the word that came to mind. Simply beautiful. He was surprised by this, since he'd never really thought of her in those terms.

She turned to him. "Hello, David. I'm sorry to keep you waiting. I was just giving my staff the afternoon off, so nobody will be using the computer while you look at it."

"I'm sure they're happy with me for getting them a little unexpected time off."

She smiled that warm, genuine smile again. "You're one of their favorite people right now."

She led him into the office where the main computer was. He looked it over. It was indeed powered by a desktop PC set up as a file server. But he'd seen never anything like it. David suppressed a laugh as he traced through her system, with thin cables running everywhere throughout the office. The hallway looked like a railroad track, with the numerous cables resembling the many lines on the poles strung alongside the rails. And anywhere there was excess cable, and there was a lot, the wire was always coiled neatly with rubber bands and tucked behind something out of sight.

After inspecting the setup, he came to the inescapable conclusion that there was no way this could work. But it did.

He already knew the answer, but he had to ask. "Who set this up?"

"I did."

David smiled and then said, "I thought Sharon said you didn't know much about computers."

"I don't," she replied. "But it needed to be done, so I learned. Sort of."

David nodded and smiled. He then asked, "So why all the wrapped-up cable?"

"I didn't know how much to buy, so I just got the longest cords I could find."

It was getting harder and harder not to laugh. But offending her—or, worse yet, hurting her feelings—was the last thing he wanted to do. He was impressed with her ingenuity and obvious tenacity as he ran her system through its paces. Self-taught and with absolutely no computer skills, she had managed to create her own network to run her business. And it worked. Pretty well, in fact.

How could he say no to helping her? In that moment, he knew he was hooked. Wednesday afternoons became the time to set up her new system.

Soon David began to realize he had dragged the task out well beyond what should have been required. What began as a simple computer favor grew into getting to know each other and, gradually, spending more and more time with each other. David was surprised to find how much he enjoyed and looked forward to their time together.

But, as the saying goes, "All good thing must come to an end." David's company decided he needed to be in Southern California to help develop new products and technologies, something he couldn't do where he was now. With no other immediate prospects for a livelihood, David and Smokey moved.

His immediate reaction was predictable. Rather than look at the positives of what lay ahead, he looked at the negative. To him, it was clear as day. He had become close to someone, and, once again, that person was taken from him. It was the story of his life. And a sad story, at that. But neither Hope nor David recognized God had His hand in the events.

Instead, they found themselves talking long-distance, a lot, and getting even better acquainted. Getting closer. So, when the assignment in California ended, David made a leap of faith. He chose to help Hope, and left the familiar and comfortable world of software development to return to North Carolina. It had become obvious to him that Hope could use help running the business aspect of her practice; something he had learned quite a lot about it during their phone calls. While he enjoyed the challenge, he especially enjoyed working closely with her. Plus, it allowed her to focus on being a dentist rather than running a business, which wasn't taught in dental school.

They made quite an effective team, providing care for an ever-growing patient base. And quite without realizing it, they did a pretty good job of taking care of each other.

If dogs could talk, Smokey would have said he was relieved. David needed someone. After all, dogs don't live forever.

MARCH 2002

American poet Delmore Schwartz once wrote, "Time is the fire in which we burn." Time spares no one. It cannot be stopped or even slowed. But it can be accelerated. Medical problems induced by a past full of abuse and neglect tend to hasten the inevitable.

Time was about to catch up with Smokey.

David liked routine in his life, which meant there was routine in Smokey's life too. Managing Smokey's care was one of David's top priorities. Smokey was that special dog David's mom had always promised him he would have. In recent months, the routine visits to Jon, David's friend and Smokey's veterinarian, had become weekly occurrences. Today was the day of the week for another visit.

David and Smokey exited the house and walked to the car. Next door, Jon's daughter, Sarah, took time from the coloring she was doing to wave to them. Her mother looked up from her work in the flower bed to call, "Hello, David, how are you? And how's that special dog of yours?"

"We're doing fine. On the way to your husband's office for Smokey's regular checkup."

Sarah came running across the lawn from next door, her long brown hair flying. "Hi, Mr. Hyler. Hi, Smokey." She knelt to hug the dog, who, for all the world, appeared to be grinning.

Noticing her artwork, David asked, "What do you have there, Sarah?"

"I made a get-well card for Smokey," she said proudly.

"Wow, that's really sweet of you." He got down on one knee to take the card and make appreciative sounds to praise it. Then, standing again, he said, "I'll read it to Smokey in the car, but I bet he wants to say thank you right now."

She hugged the big dog's neck again and whispered in his ear, "I hope you feel better. I miss playing with you. Daddy's going to take real good care of you. I love you."

As she walked back to her house, David and Smokey continued to the car. David helped Smokey into the car. "You're getting heavy, pal. We'd better ease up on the treats a bit."

As soon as they entered the vet's office, Smokey's nose went into overdrive. It was a cornucopia of smells, and the shepherd took the time to sniff and catalog each dog that had passed across the linoleum floor recently.

David checked in and then sat down to wait. Smokey lay at his feet as David lovingly stroked his fur and passed the time talking to him. Meanwhile, the other animals in the waiting area moved closer to Smokey but approached only as close as their leashes would allow. A cat in her owner's lap in the corner eyed the canines as if it would need to run for its life at any moment.

Gillian, a senior vet tech who had been with Jon ever since he'd started the practice nearly twenty years earlier, came out and called Smokey's name. She'd known David nearly as long and had taken an interest in Smokey from the day David adopted him. Her gentle smile and caring touch meant a lot to David, and he suspected Smokey sensed it all as well. They stopped at the scale for a quick weigh-in before entering the examination room.

"*Hmm*, I see my friend here has gained a pound or two."

"Funny, we were just discussing that as I put him into the car," David said.

Smokey seemed to have the most innocent "who me?" expression imaginable.

Inside the room, David grunted again as he put Smokey up on the stainless-steel examination table. "You are definitely going on a diet," he said, without any conviction that he would follow through on that statement.

Jon came into the room, dressed in a white lab coat, with his stethoscope around his neck. The natural gentleness and compassion he brought to his profession shone in the smile framed by a dark goatee. "Hi, David. How's it going, buddy?" He moved to the exam table to rub the dog's head. "Hey, Smokey, did you get to see Sarah before you came to visit with me?"

"We did, and she made Smokey a get-well card."

Jon began his examination of Smokey. "I've never seen her act that way with any other dog. Smokey is very special."

"He's very fond of Sarah too."

Jon turned back to David. "You know, you really don't need to make an appointment to come in every week. I'd be happy to walk next door."

"I know, Jon, but I don't want to take advantage of our friendship. Besides, Smokey likes getting out. With me working at home, we don't get out as much as we should, and you know how much he enjoys the ride."

"I know. But you wouldn't be taking advantage of me. Besides, what are best friends for, if not to help one another out?" As he continued to examine Smokey, Jon changed the subject. "By the way, how's it going with the young lady you met? You haven't told me much about her."

"Very well. Her name is Hope. She's a pediatric dentist who works mainly with special-needs kids. She has a four-year-old daughter named Shelby. But, most important of all, I guess, is that she puts up with me and my dog."

Continuing the exam, Jon smiled. "You don't say? Sounds like, if things work out, you'd have an instant family. And, speaking of family and your dog, tell me how you think my buddy has been doing this week."

"I could lie and tell you how great Smokey's doing, but the truth is, he's continuing to slowly and steadily go downhill—almost daily, it seems. The effects of the spinal tumor are getting more noticeable, and the lack of exercise is causing him to gain weight."

"So I noticed, as far as the weight goes." Jon reached for a set of X-rays.

"I could try to lie to you as well, but you know me too well for that to work." Jon placed the X-rays in the viewer. "Let's take a look at where we are."

David moved closer to the screen but never stopped touching Smokey, keeping his hand on the big dog's shoulder.

"I know you can read these better than most vets, including me, but humor me; I have to go through this for the record. Here's the image from two months ago." Jon put another X-ray up beside it and began to point to several key areas of Smokey's spine. "And here's the one from his last visit. You can see the progression: here, here, and down here."

David moved closer to Smokey as Jon turned to face him. They stood on either side of Smokey as they talked, both stroking the dog gently.

David swallowed hard. "How much time do we have?"

"To be honest, I have no idea. But I do know it's not long. I also know he will let you know when it's time." Jon pointed to the X-ray. "You can see how the progression is moving here and here, and as his organs start to shut down."

More and more, Jon's voice seemed to be coming from down in a well. David knew he had to hear this, but it was the last thing in the world he wanted to listen to right now. He couldn't bear the thought of yet another loss in his life.

Once back home, David sat with Smokey's head in his lap as he rubbed the dog's neck gently. Lost in thought and feeling helpless, he almost missed hearing the phone ring. Startled from his reverie, David picked it up and answered with a distracted hello.

It was Hope, calling from the conference she was attending. "Hi, sweetheart."

Her enthusiastic and bubbly attitude didn't match the way he was currently feeling. But he tried to sound positive anyway. "Hi, honey. How's Hawaii?"

"Hawaii's great! But the conference is really boring. I can't believe I'm going to have to endure these lectures for another three days."

"Are you saying you aren't getting to spend a little time on the beach? I thought the point of having a conference in a place like that is to mix in a little enjoyment."

"Oh, I am. It's a wonderful place to have a conference. I was just talking about the actual time I'm in the meetings."

"And you expect me to feel sorry for you?"

"Wel-l-l-l-l … I'm not exactly suffering just because some sessions are boring." The enthusiasm left her voice, and her tone got more serious. "But I did have one positive thing happen today."

"Really? What's that?"

"I was offered a job."

"A job? But you own your own practice. You're your own boss. What's wrong with that?

"I know, I know. It's just that this job represents everything I've wanted to do and have worked for. It even has a teaching element in a residency training program."

David was slow in answering, then quietly said, "Let me guess. You'd have to move."

"Yes, that's the tough part. It's in New England, near Boston."

David lowered the phone from his ear in frustration and laid it in his lap. He could barely hear the voice from the phone.

"Honey, are you there?" Hope was asking.

He put the receiver back to his ear. "Yeah, I'm still here in North Carolina. I just can't believe I'm going to lose you too."

There was a pause, then she said, "David, you're not going to lose me. At least let me finish. I'm not taking the job. Shelby just started school, and I'm sure not going off and leaving you. It's just nice to know that my skills are still in demand."

Silence invaded both ends of the phone.

Hope then said urgently, "Wait a minute. What do you mean … losing me too? What's happened to Smokey?"

"We had our weekly visit with Jon." David paused and cleared his throat, his voice heavy with emotion. "I'm losing him, and there's nothing I can do about it."

He paused again, and she waited for him to finish.

"One day soon, he'll just collapse. Jon said Smokey would let me know when he wanted me to let him go."

"I'm so sorry, honey," Hope said. "I know how special Smokey is to you."

"You have no idea." David couldn't help his tears. "Smokey is running out of time, and there's nothing I can do about it."

"You know, Jon is right. Smokey will let you know. Besides, sweetheart, none of us are in control of something like this."

"I know. God is the one who is really in control ... but it still hurts."

"I know it does, but remember what He says in Jeremiah 29:11: 'For I know the plans I have for you, plans for'—"

He finished it for her: "... 'good and not for evil.' I know, believe me I know, but I still struggle with that, given everything in my past. Sometimes I feel like those are just words."

"But they're good words. Don't give up on God, and you sure had better not give up on me. Neither one of us is done with you yet, and we certainly aren't leaving you."

"I know that in my head, but down deep, I can't shake the feelings of the past."

"I know, but you're not losing me. I turned the job down, so let's move past this. Please?"

David sighed. "I'm sorry, honey." He gave an unconvincing little chuckle. "You'd think that, by now, I would have moved on and left that baggage behind me. It's just the thought of losing Smokey after all we have been through together. He's been by my side no matter what. He's protected me in ways I can't even begin to describe. He's more than a dog; he's a special friend, a gift."

"Then enjoy whatever time you have left," Hope said. "If Smokey could talk, that's what he'd tell you to do. He'd rather live in the present with you than dwell on the past. I'll be home in a few days, and we can all go to the beach. I know how much he loves the beach."

"Actually, that's a good idea. I think I'll go take him for a walk now. It's a beautiful evening here."

"That's the idea. Enjoy the evening air."

"Thanks, honey. You always make me feel better."

"I try, but I suspect Smokey does a better job of it than I do. But at least I don't shed as much."

They shared a good laugh, and then Hope said, "Okay, go take your walk. I love you, and I'll call you tomorrow."

"I love you too. Good night."

David hung up the phone. Smokey was sitting there, holding his leash. "Heard the word *walk*, did you? Well, let's do it. We won't go far."

They walked down the short path to the beach. "You know, Smokey, Hope has been by my side through some of the toughest times, just like you." The dog looked up at him, as if he understood. "Maybe she's the one."

The stretch of sand was deserted at this hour. The sun hung low on the horizon, creating a ribbon of reflection on the water, framed by low clouds.

They began to absorb the peacefulness of the scene.

"Maybe it's time you had some help looking after me. What do you think?"

The shepherd seemed to nod affirmation.

"You're right. As soon as she gets back, I'll ask her."

"How would you like to be my best man? Well, okay, maybe not, but you can be my best dog. You have been that, you know."

It was a casual, strolling pace, but even so, David could see Smokey was struggling. "Looks like you're getting a little tired. Why don't we take this shortcut back to the house?"

David turned into an alley between two buildings, so they could be home in a matter of minutes. The light from the setting sun had already left this area, but the streetlights had not yet turned on. Within a few steps, David found himself in the dark, trying to avoid garbage cans, trash bags that hadn't made their way into the cans, and an occasional parked car from a nearby residence (he hoped). It was then that they came across three men breaking into one of the parked cars. By the time David realized what was going on, retreat was no longer an option.

The lead thug had already spotted David and turned to face him. "What are you looking at?"

The light at the end of the alley flickered to life in the darkness as the second man continued to work on the car. At that moment, a third man walked around from behind the car, thumping a short crowbar into the palm of his hand. Grinning in a way that seemed to use only one side of his mouth, he said, "You got a problem?"

These vandals weren't the only thing the darkness concealed. The presence of a large, black-and-tan German shepherd had gone unnoticed until Smokey stepped out from behind David into the ever-brightening shaft of light in front of him. Eyes clearly focused on the man with the crowbar, Smokey's ears were pitched forward, and the scruff on the back of his neck stood up. This was no longer a sick dog; this was an alert German shepherd prepared to defend his master.

"No, but you might," David said quietly, with confidence that he hoped would not be tested.

The men took a step back when they saw the dog. It was clear they were weighing their options and not liking the odds. "Come on guys," one of them said. "Let's get out of here."

David watched them disappear into the dark. With the sounds of their hurried footsteps growing fainter, he bent down to praise Smokey and pet him. "Good boy. You were ready to take them on, weren't you?"

He looked down the alley to ensure that they were gone. They were. "Okay, big guy, let's go home."

As he got up to go, Smokey collapsed where he was. Panic-stricken, David dropped to the ground and cradled Smokey's head in his lap. He sat there, frozen in time, as they gazed at each other. Smokey's last act was to give all he had for David. Tears began to run down David's face. "Oh no, no ... not yet ... it can't be time yet."

Smokey's eyes seemed to say otherwise as the light slowly faded and then quietly left.

David remained there for a long time, his tears falling on the coat of his beloved animal lying silently in his lap. Save for the dim light of the lone streetlamp, darkness settled softly about them.

NINE

I T HAD BEEN the longest weekend in David's memory. His young neighbor, Sarah, walked slowly across the lawn from next door. Several newspapers lay about his doorstep. Clearing a spot in the middle, she put two roses and a folded picture on the doormat, rang the doorbell, and ran away.

David came to the door, with disheveled hair and several days' growth of beard. He looked around to see who had rung the bell but saw no one. Glancing down, he noticed the flowers. He picked them up, along with the picture, and took them inside.

He gazed at the picture of Smokey on the hall table. "Looks like you got some mail, buddy." He unfolded the picture. It was a crayon drawing of Smokey in heaven.

His eyes brimmed over again. "Why do You always leave me alone and hurting like this?" He looked upward. "Why do you keep taking away the ones who love me?"

Later that afternoon, Hope came over. David met her at the door, still scraggly and unshaven.

"David, you look terrible."

"Thanks. It's good to see you too."

"You know what I mean."

"Yeah, I know. C'mon in." They walked into the kitchen, and he poured her a cup of coffee. He gave her a weak smile. "You know what? You've never said the things that bug me the most."

"What would that be?"

"That he was just a dog, or that I need to get over it."

"I know Smokey was more than a dog. He was your best friend, a companion you could count on. He just happened to have four legs. And you can't get over it until you've finished grieving."

"You get it. Most people don't."

"Yes, I get it." She put her hand on his. "That's why you shouldn't be shutting me out. I understand."

"I don't mean to shut you out."

"I know you don't."

"It's not only Smokey. It's my mother. My father. G'anny. Grandpa. And now Smokey. All those I care about the most keep disappearing from my life."

"And you haven't come to terms with any of those losses."

"No."

"Well, I wouldn't tell you to get over it, but I would say you need to come to terms with it—all of it. I wish you'd let me help."

"I've had people try to help before. They've done me no good, and neither have their words. All they do is annoy me."

"That's because there are some situations where there are no words that will do any good."

"Exactly. That's why I don't want to hear them."

Hope sighed. "That's how it is at a funeral—a whole lot of people saying meaningless words. But you have to look beyond the words and into their hearts. What they're really saying is, 'I want to share your pain.' The words don't matter. They only want to take a little piece of your grief on themselves and carry it away with them. And if you let them have that little piece, you soon discover it really is better, because so many people care. That's what I want to do. Share your pain. I don't want you to forget. I don't want to say something to make it all go away. I simply want you to let me in, so I can help carry the burden."

"I think you're wrong."

"Wrong about what?"

"About not being able to say something that helps. I think you just did."

TEN

FALL 2003

D AVID TOOK A chance. He let Hope in. Over the course of the next few months, she willingly shared David's pain. She helped carry his burden. She showed him what real love was. Day after day, week after week, month after month, Hope was there for him. Those closest to both of them saw the tremendous care and support they gave each other as their love grew and deepened. So, it was no surprise to anyone when they announced a year later that they were planning a small, private wedding. Life was good, and as David's friend Jon had predicted, he now he had a family.

Yet something was still missing. There was a hole in his life … one that even Hope couldn't fill.

David stood in the office of his house, scanning the wall of memorabilia. His eyes swept over the numerous photos documenting his past and who he was, pausing briefly on one of him back in 1967, holding a stuffed dog. He smiled, lost in the past for a moment as he reached out to tentatively touch the image of the toy. There were framed photos of him with various military awards and decorations, photos of his current family, and, almost seeming out of place, two framed crayon drawings. One was the rendition he'd done of him and his mother, and the other was the drawing his young neighbor had done for Smokey. The latter forced him to shift his attention to his desk and the framed picture of the dog. He reached out to touch it lovingly. As the memories and emotions flooded back, he picked it up and sat down in his desk chair, holding the photo in his lap.

Just then, Hope passed by the door. "I'm going to grab a snack. Are you hungry?" When she didn't get a response, she took a tentative step into the office. "David, did you hear me? What's wrong?"

David jerked his head up. "I'm sorry; I was just thinking."

"Thinking about what?"

"I dunno … maybe that I'm getting really tired of losing everything I love and care about. No matter how hard I work at it or how hard I try, I just can't save them."

Hope walked behind him and gently massaged his shoulders. "That again? I hoped we were making progress with that. Well, you're not going to lose me. Besides, it isn't up to you. You aren't the one in control."

He smiled slightly—a smile of resignation. They had been through this discussion before on a number of occasions. "I know, I know. God is the one in control, but I still hurt."

Hope moved to sit on the edge of the desk where she could face him. She took his hand in hers and leaned forward to gaze straight into the eyes. "David, Smokey is not hurting now, and I'm pretty sure he doesn't want you to hurt either. It's been well over a year. Don't you think it's time to find another dog that really needs you?"

"Yeah, I guess … I don't know … maybe."

She got up, patted his arm, and said playfully, "That's what I love about you: you're so decisive. Now that I think of it, I believe I'll pass on that snack. I'm going to go tuck Shelby in and then turn in myself. I'm seeing a lot of patients in the morning." She paused to lean down and give him a kiss. "Coming to bed?"

"Soon. I'll be there in a little while."

"Okay. Come when you're ready."

She left the room and he got up to replace the Smokey's picture on the wall. "I know she's right," he told the picture. "I know."

Not normally an early riser, David was already busy on his computer by the time the walls of the office were painted pink by the breaking dawn.

Hope came into the room, with two steaming cups of coffee. She placed one on the desk next to the computer, where he could reach it. David was looking at one dog after another on the computer screen.

"Did you come to bed last night?"

"Yes, but you were already asleep. And you didn't wake when I got up early."

She peered over his shoulder. "I see you decided to take my advice."

"Not really. Smokey said I should do this."

"You don't say." Her tone turned teasing. "Did he also tell you to clean up the mess in the garage?"

"Strangely enough, he didn't mention that."

"Why am I not surprised?"

"Cute."

"I have my moments."

He grinned. "I wasn't talking about you. I was talking about this dog. This is an award-winning shepherd."

"Really?"

"Yeah, it says here that she's won the prestigious Boomerang Award."

"Wow, that sounds impressive. What did she do to earn that? Keep bringing stuff back?"

"I suppose you could say that, only it was herself she kept bringing back."

"Huh?"

"It's the award given to the dog that is adopted and returned the most number of times."

Hope paused. "Why has she been brought back so much?"

"Simply put, I guess you'd have to say she failed. For whatever reason, she just didn't meet people's expectations, and so they didn't want her anymore."

"How sad. How many?"

"Six."

"*Hmm.* Sounds perfect for you."

"Oh, wait—it gets better. It says she's unadoptable and that she's not good with kids."

"Like I said, honey, just the kind of challenge you need. Sounds perfect."

Hope moved toward the door, leaving him staring at the screen. From the doorway, Hope asked, "By the way, what's her name?"

"Cadie."

As Hope's footsteps faded down the hall, David heard her say, "Pretty name."

Staring even more intently at the screen, he said, "So, Cadie, what's your story?"

ELEVEN

DAVID MIGHT HAVE understood the situation better if he had actually seen for himself the run-down house in a low-income neighborhood. As a police cruiser pulled up to the curb and the two officers got out of the car, they heard the barking and whining of a dog behind the house. They were immediately met by a young woman with several young children in tow. The driver stayed by the car as his partner walked toward the woman.

"Are you the one who phoned in the complaint?" the officer asked.

The woman looked tired, and the kids now flanking her might have been the reason. "Yeah, I did. 'Bout time you got here. This is the third time he's threatened me and my kids."

"Who threatened you?"

"My landlord." She pointed to the back of the house, where all the barking was coming from. "He lives back there. All I asked him to do was to keep that dog quiet. It barks all the time, night and day."

"Ma'am, did he threaten you?"

She put her hand on her hip and nodded. "He said if I didn't shut up, he wouldn't be responsible for what happened next."

"Was he specific as to what he meant by that?"

She shook her head. "I told you just what he said it. But knowing him, he'll use his dog and make it attack us. Are you going to do something or not? He's crazy. Ask anyone. We're all scared to say anything 'cause he'll kick us out, but this is too much. My little boy wasn't hurting anyone; he was just playing in the yard."

"We'll go over and talk to the man."

"So, you aren't going to—"

"One step at a time, ma'am. We have to take one step at a time." He walked over to the car.

"You want animal control here?" the other officer asked.

"That wouldn't be a bad idea."

The driver reached for the police radio's microphone. "This is A-264."

"Go ahead, A-264." The dispatcher's voice sounded thin and remote on the small speaker.

"We need animal control at 136 Elm Street."

"Copy that."

The two officers walked around to the back, picking their way through the trash in the yard and on the porch. The barking increased dramatically in volume and intensity as they knocked on the door.

A voice came from behind the door. "Cadie, shut up! Who is it?"

"It's the police, sir. Can you open the door?"

"Whatcha want?"

"Can you step outside for a moment, sir? We just want to talk to you."

"Get lost. I didn't do nuthin' wrong."

"Sir, open the door, and step outside. All we want to do is talk with you."

The door opened to reveal a man in his undershirt, holding a baseball bat loosely by his side. The smell of alcohol was strong, and the man seemed to be having trouble focusing.

The officers put their hands on their weapons but did not draw them. "Sir, put the bat down. We only want to talk."

"I didn't do nuthin'," the man said, his speech slurred. He raised the bat, holding it in both hands in front of him.

"Put the bat down, sir."

"I'm not putting the bat down." He made a wild flinging gesture intended to point the way away from his house. "Get off my property."

Moving so fast that the man didn't have time to react, both officers grabbing him and pulled him out the door. The bat clattered across the porch as they dropped him facedown, snapping handcuffs on his wrists.

"You're under arrest."

"You can't do this to me," the man protested.

"Sir, I'm placing you under arrest for assault on a police officer."

"But I didn't—"

"You announced your intention to do so, and you brandished a weapon. We aren't required to wait until you actually hit us."

"Haven't you guys got something better to do? Leave me alone, and get off my property."

The barking inside the house reached a fever pitch, but as the officers looked around, the animal wasn't visible inside the darkened house. Pulling the man to his feet, they took him down the steps and through the crowd that had gathered to watch. Neighbors applauded as the trio headed toward the cruiser.

Just then, a van marked Animal Control arrived. When the man saw this, he started swearing, then added, "That's my dog. You don't touch her. You leave Cadie alone."

The officers tucked the man in the backseat of the cruiser, placing a hand on his head to ensure that he didn't hit his head. As the lead officer leaned in to read him his rights, the driver turned to the animal-control officers, gestured toward the house, and said, "It's all yours."

The two animal-control officers approached the yard, carrying two poles with loops on the ends and lines from the loops feeding back to the poles. They entered the yard and surveyed the area.

"Whew!" one said. "Can you believe that smell?"

"And the mess. How can anything live in this?"

"I can't stand this. Let's just get the dog and get out of here."

"There it is."

"I think the guy said it was a she."

The shepherd was black with minimal brown markings, and she was all but invisible standing in the shadows.

"Whatever. There she is, over there."

"Okay, look at the hair standing on the back of her neck and the way she's holding her ears. You know what that means—she's wired and ready for action. We gotta get these loops on the first pass, or she's likely to be out of here, and then we'll have to chase her all over the place."

The dog tried to bolt past them. The first officer missed with the loop, but the second made a catch, nearly having it pulled from his hands as the weight of the dog hit the end. The dog spun, trying to pull away, and the second officer slipped his loop over the dog's head, securing the animal between them. Cautiously, they led her away to put her in the back of the van.

Someone in the crowd said, "What's going to happen to that poor dog?"

The person next to him said, "Poor dog? You've got to be kidding. I don't know and don't care what happens to it. It's gone, and we can finally have some peace and quiet. Besides, who would want something like that anyway?"

Back at Animal Control, they were every bit as cautious getting her into a cage.

As they hung up their catch sticks, the first officer said, "I just got off the phone with German Shepherd Rescue. She'll be off our hands by this time tomorrow."

"I'm a little surprised they accepted her."

"Well, I didn't feel obligated to tell them everything I know about her."

"Good thinking. I wasn't looking forward to trying to walk this one."

Had David been able to see that scene, to see that environment, he would have better understood how it could have been the springboard to set in motion the subsequent unsuccessful placements. He scrolled through the data available on the animal, but that information didn't tell him nearly as much as actually seeing the scene would have done.

Nevertheless, his heart had been touched. Truth be told, he was surprised by just how much. Her eyes, like Smokey's, had a depth that he couldn't quite figure out. It was as if they called to him. They were compelling. With that, David picked up the phone to make the call. He knew the number very well, having volunteered to help there for years. Getting the head of the rescue on the phone, David pushed back in his chair to have a heart-to-heart about beginning the process to bring home a dog that nobody wanted … or believed in.

Occasionally, a dog might be returned once or twice, but Cadie had been returned a record six times! Because of that, she'd been assigned the status of permanent foster. That meant she'd spend the rest of her life moving from one foster home to another: cared for, but never knowing a true home. She was unwanted, unadoptable, and unacceptable. Something David knew all too well.

Still, he was cautions. Smokey had set the bar very high. They had bonded immediately, clicked from the very first moment. Could lightning really strike twice? Could another German shepherd do that?

"Only one way to find out," he said aloud as he picked up his keys and headed out.

David found the house easily. The neighborhood had been built back in the 1950s, so the houses all had a distinctive look. Before pulling up the driveway, he double-checked the address—though that was unnecessary, if the sound of dogs barking was any indication. As he got of the car, he noticed an older woman coming out the door. Blue jeans and a sweatshirt, both with a fair amount of dirt of them, made it look like she'd been working in the yard. David knew it was probably with the dogs he could hear barking and not gardening.

The woman stepped toward him and extended her hand. "Hi. You must be David. I'm Chris. Rescue called and said you were coming."

Interesting, thought David. *No pleasantries—straight to the point.*

"Good to meet you," he said.

Chris looked over her shoulder, toward the back the house where the barking was coming from, and then brought her gaze back to David.

David wondered which bark belonged to Cadie.

Chris grimaced a bit and rubbed the back of her neck. "Look, they tell me you're really good with these dogs, but this one … well, I think she's beyond anyone's help. Frankly, I think you're wasting your time."

Definitely straight to the point. Maybe even a bit beyond it, David thought as he nodded. "I might be, but may I at least see her?"

Chris stared at him for a moment and then sighed. Reluctantly, she said, "Okay. But let me put the others up before I let her out. You can go around the side of the house, and I'll meet you out back."

With that, Chris stepped back inside and abruptly shut the door, leaving David standing on the steps, somewhat taken aback by the greeting and apparent attitude. After a brief moment, he did as he'd been instructed and stepped around the side to the back of the house. There, he found Chris calling four German shepherds of various coloration and age into the house. This calmed them, and the barking immediately ceased.

Chris motioned for David to join her. "I keep her in the laundry room to avoid problems with the others."

"What kind of problems?"

"She doesn't seem to like other dogs much, or cats for that matter. Oh, and not too fond of people, especially small ones. Not sure how she is with fish, though. Never put one in with her." She gave a nervous laugh. "You might want to stand back."

Chris opened the door.

The dog froze in the doorway when she saw David, and then she began to slowly step outside. She kept her head down but never lost eye contact with David. She didn't appear scared. Her ears were up, and by all outward appearances, she was simply being cautious. With a slightly nervous look, she gave him a wide circle, trying to ignore him. *Wary*—that was the word. It was definitely not the greeting he'd received from other dogs. This girl had no confidence and was unsure of everything—including herself. This meant she'd react from fear, not confidence. One red flag went up for him.

Chris shrugged. "Why don't I let you two get acquainted? I'll be over there if you need me." She pointed to the far corner of the yard. "I'll be over here if you need me."

"Thanks." David turned to study the dog. She was nervously walking first one way and then the other, watching him closely, without appearing to look at him at all. *Antisocial*—that's what the file had said. He could see why she was being kept from the other dogs. That was not healthy or normal. Flag number two!

But he had driven almost an hour to come take a look at this dog, so David decided to take charge. He started talking to her—calmly but firmly. "They tell me you're a loner." He sat on a stump in the yard. "I can identify with that. I've been there myself."

With David no longer standing, the dog ceased to pace but still did not approach.

"In fact, I'm still that way a lot of the time, until Hope forces me out of it. Hope is my wife, by the way. Maybe you and I can help each other out. What do you think?" David remained calm as spoke and kept his movements very small and simple. Everything he was doing was intended to calm this dog and establish trust through a nonthreatening exchange. Voice was important, but so, too, was body language. Subtle movements, like moving a foot closer, shifting his weight on the stump, or holding out his hand, could have significant impact.

Cadie watched him, cocking her head. Her body language improved, so his soft, reassuring tone was obviously helping. For each action that David took, she reacted with increasing trust.

"I also hear you're antisocial. That's going to be a problem, because that's just not healthy for any of God's creatures, no matter how many legs they have."

Cadie lay down, still watching him closely. In a slow, easy move, David slid off the stump and went down on one knee. "Come here, sweetheart. Let's talk."

Slowly, tentatively, she came up to him. He looked her right in the eyes. There, he saw the real Cadie—a sweet girl looking for a place to call home, a German shepherd wanting to serve. A different set of descriptors came to mind—*bright, intelligent, longing, hopeful*—in a word, *special*. In seconds, he was sure this would work out fine.

"They've all been wrong about you, haven't they?" He reached out a hand to scratch her behind the ear. "You and I both know that's not God's plan." He paused a moment and then asked, "How about we go for a walk?"

David stood slowly, picked up a nearby lead, and snapped it on her collar. She didn't appear to mind. He took a few steps with her, and she followed along naturally. "You're going to be fine. Now, I, on the other hand, am still a work in progress. You'll need to be patient with me, okay?"

Several minutes later, Chris came back over to where they were circling the yard. "I wouldn't have believed it if I hadn't seen it myself. No one's been able to do that with this dog."

"She's fine."

"There's normally a two-week trial period, but they said over at the rescue that you get anything you want."

His voice was firm. "I want her."

David loaded Cadie into the car, then turned and eyed her. She was lying on the seat, looking uncomfortable.

"Not fond of car rides, huh? I get that. Every time you get in a car, you go somewhere and don't come back, right? Well, that'll change after you make a few trips where you end up coming home after each of them. Are you hungry?" David paused as if expecting her to answer. No response, not even a physical one. "Well, I am. How do you feel about a hamburger?"

Twenty minutes later, they arrived at one of David's favorite fast-food restaurants: Burger King. *Probably best to use the drive-through,* he thought. "Now this is a rare treat, Cadie. Don't expect this all the time. I'm pretty strict with diet, but this is a special occasion. You can think of it as a combination birthday and Christmas present."

"May I take your order please?" the thin voice from the box said.

"One birthday cake wrapped as a Christmas present. To go, please."

"Excuse me?"

"Sorry, private joke. I'll have the number three, and my companion will have a burger meal. Make that with an iced tea and a bowl of water, please."

"Excuse me? A bowl of what?"

"Let's just say a cup of water with no ice."

She told him the amount of the order, adding, "Pull to the window, please."

David drove forward. The moment the window opened, Cadie barked.

The girl jerked back instinctively. "He startled me."

"He is a she. She's just being protective of me, seeing someone so close to the car when she didn't see you coming. She's a little nervous now, but she really likes the food here." *I hope.*

He handed over the money, and the girl disappeared back inside to retrieve the food. "Cadie, we're going to have to work on your social skills a bit. This is as good a place as any to start. School's in session, and training begins now."

The window opened again, and Cadie barked. She then tried to lunge over David's left shoulder as the hand and the food came in. David expected this and brought his up arm to simultaneously block her movement and hold her back. He then calmly took the food with his right hand. The girl, visibly shaken, quickly counted her fingers, then closed the window. Cadie, perhaps for the first time, had been firmly corrected.

"Yes, we definitely need to acquaint you with the K-9 version of Emily Post."

David drove to a nearby park. He got out slowly and went around to her door. "Let's see if I can do this without you bolting and running, or me spilling our food." Without opening the door very wide, he carefully snapped the leash onto her collar and led her out with his left hand, holding the food and drinks in his right.

They walked through the grass and over a small bridge that spanned a creek, continuing until they found a quiet spot away from everyone. He sat down, followed by Cadie. She was watching him with interest as he slowly unwrapped the food. Her eyes locked on the hamburger.

"*Hmm.*" With a small chuckle, he continued. "Looks like I have your undivided attention now."

He broke off a piece of hamburger and gave it to her. "So, sweetheart, we're going to have to figure out how to make this work."

Her eyes were bright with interest as he gave her another bite. "They've said a lot of things about you that just aren't true about German shepherds. And I'm pretty sure they aren't true about you."

He took a bite of his burger, then gave her another piece of hers. It went down her mouth like he'd dropped it down a gopher hole. "You wouldn't consider chewing that a little, would you?" He grinned. "I have to say, after that little incident at the drive-through, I'm not completely sure about you. You didn't like her perfume, right? Is that it? I guess if I were you, I'd have done the same thing."

His bonding exercise by means of food seemed to be working. He then pulled the top off the cup of water and gave her a drink, followed by another morsel of her treat. "All right, house rules: You can get on any piece of furniture you want, but if you tell anybody I said that, I'll deny it. Hope doesn't want you on the couch. She'll probably give in on the bed, but the couch is another story. Everything but the couch is fair game."

Cadie gave a small *whuff*.

"Sorry. Too much time between bites, huh? All right. Here. Okay, topic two is health care. You don't need to worry about it. Whatever you need, you're going to get. I've got some great doctors on my team, including my best friend and neighbor, and they're going to take good care of you."

David took another bite of his burger. "One more thing, and this is really important. We've got a little girl at home. Her name is Shelby. She's a very special girl, just like you are. You absolutely *have* to promise me that you two are going to get along. We are *not* going to have any issues here. You two are going to be buddies, okay? She's looking forward to meeting you, and I think it would be wonderful for the two of you to grow up together."

He reached his hand toward her. She looked at it disdainfully, as it held no food.

"Okay? Have we got a deal? Shake?"

She didn't bring up her paw.

"We're going to have to work on that too. You just be good with Shelby. You've finished your burger … what more do you want? The tater tots? Just let me—"

He looked at the dog.

"Oh, for Pete's sake. All right, here."

TWELVE

DAVID BROUGHT CADIE into the house. Shelby, delighted and all smiles, started to run to the dog, who reacted by backing up, unsure of what was going on. But, before Shelby could take another step, Hope caught her and reeled her back.

"She's nervous right now, sweetheart," Hope said. "Remember what we talked about yesterday? We have to get acquainted with her slowly."

"Sorry, Mommy ... I forgot."

Hope knelt down by the child and held out her hand. David let out Cadie's leash slowly, and she moved forward to smell Hope's hand.

"Can you do that?" she said to Shelby.

Shelby held out a tiny hand and giggled as Cadie smelled it, then licked it.

Hope laughed. "I think there may still be a little pancake syrup on her hands."

The licking and the giggling continued.

"Couldn't have done anything better if you had planned it," David said.

The other hand got a good cleansing as well. David then took Shelby and Cadie to a quiet corner of the living room, where a crate sat. "This is her safe zone," he said. "This is where she is going to come when she gets nervous. We don't want to violate that. Don't bang on the cage; don't make any sudden movements around it when she's in here. Anytime she's nervous, this is her spot. This is the one place where no human is allowed."

Cadie sniffed the crate but did not go in.

"Okay, I'm going to let her off the leash now and let her explore a little."

Off the leash now, Cadie moved into the living room, sniffing and exploring to get a sense of where she was.

Shelby went to her room to play, leaving Hope and David alone to talk about this first meeting. They went into the kitchen and poured cups of coffee.

"So, how did the pickup go?" Hope said.

"It went well, except for a girl she nearly scared to death at a drive-through. Fortunately, the attendant still has all her fingers."

"What happened?"

"Cadie lunged at the arm coming from the drive-through window. I'm not sure if it was the arm or the food, or what it was, but it wasn't a good reaction."

Hope's eyes locked with his. "Tell me the truth. How do you feel about her?"

"I'll be honest. I'm not sure. I'm a little more concerned because of the incident at the drive-through than I was when I first met her. I called Jon from the car to get his thoughts."

"And?"

"He sounds like you. He said that if anyone could turn this dog around, it was me, and that he couldn't tell me anything about shepherds I don't already know. But he did warn me to be careful."

They heard the *click-click-click* of the dog's toenails as she came across the kitchen floor to lie down in front of the center island. Soon David glanced over to see that Shelby had slipped back into the room to peek at the dog from behind a half wall separating the living room from the kitchen. Playfully, she smiled at Cadie, then quickly dropped out of sight.

Hope looked very concerned. "That doesn't make me feel too comfortable. How do you think she's going to be with Shelby? I mean, bringing a dog in here that you're not completely comfortable with is more than I bargained for."

David held up his hands, as if to ward off her words. "I know, I know. Look, for now, they shouldn't be left alone together. We need to keep an eye on them. Until we're certain, we need to ensure that one of us is always around anytime Cadie is out of her kennel, and if there's ever a problem, that's where we need to put Cadie immediately."

Shelby popped up at a slightly different place on the half wall. David and Hope didn't notice. But Cadie did. Her eyes brightened, and her ears perked up.

"Cadie has to understand that spot is her safe zone. It's how we're able to control the situation until she bonds with us and begins to trust us. I'm not concerned once that bonding occurs, but until that happens, nothing is going to go very well. It could be a rocky period of time."

This wasn't helping Hope's concern. "Just how rocky?"

His voice was quiet. "I don't know."

Engrossed in their conversation, neither David nor Hope saw Shelby walk over toward the crate. But Cadie paid close attention.

"And how long do you think it'll take her to bond?"

David raised his hands in exasperation, then let them fall. He and Hope had talked about this before even considering another dog. "I don't know. Every dog is different."

"I don't care about that." Her voice was tense. "I care about our daughter, and you should too."

"I am, honey, I am!" Trying to calm a situation that never should have gotten this far in the first place, he paused before continuing. "Look, with Smokey, it was instantaneous. But with Cadie's background, I don't know, it might take weeks … maybe a month." He rested his head in his hands and quietly said, more to himself than Hope, "But, after what I saw today, it might take a miracle."

Shelby slipped over to Cadie's crate, smiling as she turned to look at the dog again.

Hope shook her head vigorously. "I'm not comfortable hoping for a miracle when our daughter's safety is at stake."

"I know that. Neither am I," he said sadly. "You know I wouldn't jeopardize Shelby for anything. We can't take anything for granted. We're going to have to keep a close eye on them."

The dog watched as Shelby approached the kennel.

Hope gave a deep sigh. "You don't think Cadie would actually hurt her, do you?"

David shrugged. "I don't know. She's physically capable of doing some serious damage. I don't think she would, but—"

"I'm having second thoughts about letting this dog stay, David."

"But Hope—"

"But nothing. You know I support you and Cadie, but this is more serious than I realized, particularly if it even has you nervous. What am I supposed to think? If it's going to take a miracle for this to happen, it had better happen soon, because—"

Just then, Shelby crawled into the crate, and it rattled, drawing the attention of her parents. There, in the living room, where there was supposed to be a dog, was a crate holding a little girl. Before they could react, Cadie got up and ran to the crate.

In one voice, they yelled, "Cadie! No!"

Time stood still as they watched Cadie lunge into the crate.

Then, it happened. Miraculously, Cadie simply curled up next to Shelby. As David and Hope exchanged disbelieving looks, Shelby reached out to pull the door shut and lay her head down on the big dog.

They were afraid to move, afraid they would startle the animal into reacting.

"David—"

"Just be very, very still."

Cadie was alert, processing the threat, trying to determine what was going on.

"David, you have to do something!"

"Shh! She isn't making any aggressive signs yet. And neither should we."

"Yet?!" Hope whispered fiercely. "What are you going to do? Wait until she attacks, and then try to stop it?"

Cadie brought her head closer to the child, and Hope's hand went to her mouth as she caught her breath.

Then, Cadie sniffed the small girl curiously. This tickled her ear, and Shelby brought a hand up to scratch. Cadie sniffed the delicate little hand too, which produced more giggles, but Shelby just closed her eyes and snuggled closer.

Cadie relaxed, curled into a ball around the child, and put her head on Shelby's leg. She closed her eyes to join the child in sleep.

"I don't believe it!" David let out the breath he didn't know he was holding.

"I think we just witnessed our first miracle," Hope said.

David looked up toward the ceiling. "Thank You, God."

Sitting by the crate, David kept a constant vigil as he allowed the two new friends a short nap. It was still early to be completely trusting.

After a half hour, he turned to Hope. "Honey, I'd like to try something."

He turned back to the kennel and began to gently wake the sleeping beauties and open the door. "Cadie, Shelby, would you two like to go to the park?"

Shelby was wide awake instantly. "Yes!"

"Easy, honey ... don't startle Cadie."

He looked into the cage. "Cadie, would you like to go for a walk?"

First Shelby, and then Cadie, came out. David showed Cadie the leash and moved slowly around her as he approached her head and neck. She sat quietly as he snapped the leash on her collar.

"What are you going to do?" Hope asked.

"I have a hunch. We'll be back soon."

"You keep a close eye on them. After all, it wasn't long ago we were thinking—"

"Don't worry. I'll keep Shelby safe." Then, to both child and dog, he said, "Come on, you two, let's take a walk."

At the park, Shelby immediately began to run and play, but never far away. While Cadie stayed close by David's side, she was constantly surveying her surroundings to make sure everything was all right. Every squeal from Shelby brought extra focus to Cadie. "Just as I suspected— typical German shepherd, guarding her flock." David continued to watch

Cadie's behavior very closely. The more he did that, the more he was convinced someone had totally misjudged this dog's potential.

When Shelby tired and came over to sit on the bench, Cadie, maintaining her vigil, lay down at the child's feet.

"Very interesting." David smiled. "Very interesting indeed."

David returned to the house with a sleeping Shelby on his shoulder. Cadie walked alongside on her lead.

"How did it go?" Hope asked.

"You wouldn't believe it. Cadie is being very maternal with Shelby."

Somewhat shocked, Hope responded, "Maternal? You mean motherly?"

"That's a good way to describe it. She's looking after her as if she's one of her own, as if she is her flock. She never lost track of her and was always looking around, as if protecting a lamb. Let me show you. Watch this."

He carried Shelby into her bedroom and lay her on the bed. They watched as Cadie immediately jumped up on the bed but didn't snuggle next to her. She picked a position between Shelby and the door, lay her head down, and looked toward the door, as if on guard.

"Wow!" Hope said. "I guess she *is* good with kids."

"With our kid, at least."

"Thank You, God."

"Amen. I'm not surprised. It's the nature of shepherds. Jon was telling me about one that was in a family that was having a lot of trouble. When an argument broke out between the parents, the dog would herd the two young daughters back to their bedroom and stand guard between them and the door."

"Really?"

"Not only that, he'd get in between the two when they were fighting, leaning on them to push them apart, trying to stop the argument."

"I had no idea."

"Most people don't. Shepherds are a great family breed that has suffered a lot from stereotyping and discrimination."

This was shaping up to be a great summer in the Hyler household.

THIRTEEN

F ALL WAS BEGINNING to show itself with the occasional early morning frost and brightly colored leaves in the trees. After three months, David was getting increasingly frustrated as he tried to work with Cadie. Shelby was close by, on the driveway, drawing with some colored chalk. She seemed to be on a personal mission to add even more color to the neighborhood, and the driveway was a great canvas for a budding artist.

As the days were still pleasant, Hope and David liked to keep the windows opens for the fresh air. So, it was easy for Shelby to overhear her daddy say, "Come on, Cadie, work with me. Work with me just a little bit; help me out."

Shelby called, "Daddy, come and see my drawing."

"Just a minute, sweetie," he answered. "Remember, we've got to get ready to meet Mommy at the office. She should be wrapping up right about now, so we'll pick her up and then go out to dinner." He put his hands on his hips and sighed. "All right, girl," he told Cadie. "I guess we'll give up on it for today and pick it up tomorrow. Go get yourself some water while I go look at Shelby's artwork."

He stepped outside and walked over to his young artist's sidewalk studio to look at her latest creations. "That's very good, honey. I love the colors!" Looking up at the sky, he added, "I hope it doesn't rain. I'd like Mommy to see this too."

Shelby beamed with pride.

"Oh, I almost forgot. I need to clean out the backseat of the car because we're going to try to take Cadie with us today too."

Shelby squealed in delight and began picking up her art supplies. Meanwhile, David got busy cleaning papers and trash out of the car. Cadie had gotten her drink and was looking out the window at Shelby. No one noticed the stranger.

A man dressed in a disheveled suit and carrying a briefcase had begun walking up the drive. David caught a glimpse of him through the rear window of the car, but the man obviously didn't see him, for he said, "Hi, little girl. Is your mommy or daddy home?"

David wasn't the only one who saw the man. As David stepped in view of the stranger, he realized he was one step too slow. In the same instant, he heard the screen door bang open. Cadie had opened the screen door latch, leaped from the porch, ignoring all eight steps, and bolted out to a spot about six feet in front of Shelby, between her and the stranger, who stopped immediately, shocked and frightened. And Cadie did all this without making a sound.

Cadie stared at the man. It was a no-nonsense look—all business. No teeth, no growl, as neither one was needed. She had eye contact, and that was all that was needed. She then slowly sat down, continuing to stare at the man. Her quiet confidence spoke one message far louder than words: that she'd protect her charge if she thought it necessary.

David took it all in as he approached. This protectiveness was true to the breed. He also knew shepherds would do whatever was necessary if they thought their charge was being threatened. Which was not something he needed to happen right now.

"Hi there," David said with a sense of relaxed confidence he didn't feel. "Stand real still, no sudden movements. You'll be okay." Then, under his breath, he added, "I hope."

"Absolutely" was all the man could muster in a very quiet and nervous tone. He was shaking just a bit.

David then walked up to the man and stood between him and Cadie. *Just in case,* he told himself.

The stranger was desperately trying to recall his sales pitch. Instead, all he could get out was, "Uh … well, I'm t-trying to s-sell some magazines, to raise money. Can I j-just give you some of this information?"

"No, thanks. We're not interested, and we prefer not to be solicited. What I would suggest is that you slowly walk back down the driveway. No sudden movements, and don't turn your back. Just back up slowly."

"Absolutely." The salesman did as he was instructed until he reached the end of the driveway, where he simply turned and ran.

Relieved, David smiled. "Well, Cadie, what other surprises do you have for me?" He held out his hand to his daughter. "C'mon, Shelby, let's get in the car and go get Mommy. We can tell her about today's miracle." He fastened her in her seat, then said, "Come on, Cadie, let's go for a ride."

Meanwhile, Hope sat at her desk, finishing up charts for the day. The intercom buzzed. "Doctor, I'm sorry to bother you, but there's a child out here who's in a lot of pain. I knew you'd want to see him."

"Of course. Set up exam room three, and I'll be right there." She put down the charts. Dinner would just have to wait.

Hope heard the boy before she even got to the room. She opened the door to see a ten-year-old screaming at the top of his lungs. He squirmed and pulled away, refusing to let Hope examine him. His mom and dad were concerned and confused; they had been trying to calm him, without success.

The mom continued to try, getting in Hope's way until she said, "Please, I need you to have a seat, relax, and be a silent observer."

The boy continued to fend off Hope's efforts to examine his mouth. She looked at the parents. "What happened? How long has this been going on?"

"For over an hour now. Nothing we do seems to help."

David pulled up outside Hope's office. He snapped a leash on Cadie, and they headed for the door. "Let's see if Mommy is ready," he said to Shelby.

Just before they entered the building, Shelby asked, "Do you think Mommy will be mad if we bring Cadie in with us?"

"No, honey, it's after patient hours. Mommy is just finishing up her paperwork. There's a lot of paperwork involved with being a dentist.

Besides, the staff is probably gone too. I don't see any of their cars in the parking lot."

David noticed Cadie's ears were standing upright like radar antennas. This was a new place, after all, and she was paying attention to her surroundings, as usual. Besides, as he'd just told Shelby, no one was in the office except Hope. So, holding tightly to the leash wasn't a thought that entered his mind. Which was something he was about to regret—right after he heard a little boy screaming—because just as soon as they walked in, Cadie pulled loose from David and took off down the hall.

David and Shelby followed in hot pursuit.

"Cadie, stop!" David yelled in vain.

"Cadie, *no!*" hollered Shelby with equal effect.

The dog didn't slow at all. She ran straight into the exam room, toward the sound of the screaming, which was Hope's young patient. The boy's parents gasped in shock. More accurately, the mother screamed. The only one not flustered was Cadie. She simply sat down next to the little boy. Hope, to her credit and training, remained focused on caring for her patient.

David raced around the corner. "I'm sorry, I didn't—"

Hope immediately held up her hand. "Isn't she so soft?" she murmured to the boy.

Everyone watched in silence as the screaming stopped, and the boy reached over to pet Cadie. The dog did not pull away but simply leaned against him as he caressed her ear.

The boy seemed mesmerized by the dog, allowing Hope to do the full exam. Without the boy struggling, she quickly found and treated the problem, bringing instant relief.

Right before the parents and the patient exited, the parents thanked Hope. "You were wonderful! And your dog was amazing! She's an angel in a fur coat."

Fortunately, no one saw David's reaction of disbelief.

After they'd left, Hope turned to David. "I agree with them. That was amazing." She turned and headed back to her office to close up for the evening. Over her shoulder, she added, "What we have here is a therapy dog."

Disbelief returned to David's face. "A what? A therapy dog? Are you kidding me? Where'd you get that?"

"I've read articles in several medical journals about the increased use of therapy dogs in clinical settings such as this. They've proved to be very effective, particularly with special-needs children."

"But I can't even train her to sit, much less do anything else. Until she bonds with me, there isn't any chance of doing therapy work, much less getting even basic obedience under control."

"Why not?"

"I don't know what her problem is. She just follows her own instincts."

"She sounds like you. That's why you're so good with these dogs. You don't listen to what the world says. You listen to what God tells you. He's blessed you with a gift that everybody but you can see. You need to use it."

"But she doesn't pay any attention to me."

"Maybe you should be paying attention to her. We just saw our second miracle."

"Actually," he said with a grin, "it was the third. Did I tell you the one about the traveling salesman?"

Shelby was asleep by the time they got home. Hope carried her into the house as David brought Cadie. "I'm going to put Shelby to bed," Hope said. "I'll be back in a few minutes."

"Okay."

He walked the dog into the living room and put her in the kennel, leaving the door open. Her actions were still on his mind. David lay down on the floor just outside her kennel. It was time for a heart-to-heart talk with a small measure of pleading thrown in.

"Sweetheart, when are you going to trust me? I trust you." He paused. They were looking each other right in the eye. Clearly, he had her attention, as her gaze never wavered, even when Hope walked into the room.

He continued. "Your instincts are phenomenal. Better than any shepherd I've ever seen—or even heard of, for that matter. But you have to trust me. We've got to get on the same page here. You have to work with me."

She cocked her head slightly as they continued to stare at each other. "Can you do that? I really need you to."

She then lay her head down on her paws but did not let go of his eyes, as if to say, "Let me think about it … I'll get back to you on that."

David accepted the I'm-done-listening gesture and decided to end the one-way conversation. "Well, you go to sleep now. And I'll tell you the same thing I tell Shelby: Come get me if you need me. Sleep tight."

With that David, got up and joined Hope, and they went to get ready for bed.

It had been a long day full of surprises. Both Hope and David were exhausted as they stumbled into the bedroom. After saying good night and a quick kiss, both turned onto their sides to go to sleep.

Meanwhile, downstairs, Cadie had watched the humans leave the room. They were such an interesting breed. They fascinated her. She put her head down, but sleep wouldn't come. She was intensely curious. Where did they go when they left her like this?

After lying there for a while, she followed the scent down the darkened hall. With her keen sense of smell, it was easy to follow their steps up the stairs and down the hall to the bedroom. The door was closed but not latched, and she pushed it open with her head. She came around the bed and cocked her head toward David. She got close to his face to sniff him, but he was sound asleep and didn't wake. Inches from his face, she watched him sleep. This man evoked strange feelings in her, ones she hadn't had before.

She padded around to look at Hope, finding her asleep too. She sniffed her face as well, but Hope didn't awaken either.

Cadie moved to the end of the bed. She didn't want to be alone in her kennel; she wanted to be with this man. But should she? There was a big, inviting space unused right between them. She started back out the door, and stopped. She paused to look back. He had been nothing but good to her. She could trust him. She needed to be with him and watch over him, as he did for her. She turned to jump up on the bed to curl up next to David.

The movement of the bed awoke Hope, and she rolled over to see David, sound asleep, with his arm around Cadie.

She smiled and whispered, "David."

He opened his eyes to see Cadie next to him. "Well, my goodness, what do we have here?"

Hope continued to smile as she said softly, "That's miracle four. Now you can start that training."

FOURTEEN

D AVID SIPPED HIS morning coffee as he read a through a wealth of training material and guidelines. The American Kennel Club (AKC) had provided him with the guidelines for earning the Canine Good Citizen (CGC) title: the first step to becoming a therapy dog. As he learned. the CGC Program teaches good manners to dogs and responsible dog ownership to their owners. He went on to read in the literature that the AKC's Canine Good Citizen test includes the following ten steps:

1. Accepting a friendly stranger
2. Sitting politely for petting
3. Appearance and grooming
4. Going out for a walk (walking on a loose lead)
5. Walking through a crowd
6. Sitting, going down on command, and staying in place
7. Coming when called
8. Reacting to other dogs
9. Reacting to distraction
10. Supervised separation

David spent several hours reading through all the information and test criteria to make sure he understood exactly what Cadie needed to learn and demonstrate. By lunchtime, he was ready to begin, and he took Cadie out into the yard. Class had begun.

Over the next six weeks, David worked with her every day, taking her through the exercises, checking them off one at a time in the book. Through it all, Cadie was alert, cocking her head as he talked to her, seemingly eager to please.

Today was the day. It was time for her to prove her worth and pass her test! He took her out and ran her through the steps one more time before heading to the testing center. After he signed in and filled out the paperwork at the testing center, he waited until a man in a suit with an AKC name badge came up to him. As Cadie went through her paces, David was elated, happy with how well she was doing. But the man kept shaking his head, writing notes on his clipboard.

At the end of the test, the man came over, muttered a halfhearted "Sorry," and handed him a piece of paper. Marked simply at the bottom was one word: "Failed."

David was too stunned to be devastated.

Once they were back home, he related the incident to Hope.

"I don't get it. Why did she fail?" Hope asked.

"Yeah, daddy," Shelby echoed. "She's really smart."

Looking down at Cadie, who was lying by his feet, David said, "You're right. Cadie is absolutely brilliant. Her handler, on the other hand, doesn't have a clue what he's doing. At least, according to the test we took."

"What does that mean?"

"It means I let her down. We failed with flying colors because of me. She did everything she was supposed to do; they just didn't like how she did it. Apparently, the way she has to do things doesn't have anything to do with how she's actually going to be working."

"What are you going to do?"

"Start over. We have to do it again. This time, we're going to learn to do it their way. Then, when she passes, we're going to go back to doing it the right way!" David turned to look at Cadie and said, "You are going to be the best therapy dog ever."

Start over, they did. And in less than three weeks, she was ready to take the test again. And so was David. Unfortunately, the paperwork process behind the scenes to issue her certificate for passing didn't move as fast. He'd been told to allow two to six weeks, which seemed like an eternity. Waiting by the mailbox became a daily ritual. Today was no different as he went to retrieve the mail before the postal truck made its next stop.

David sorted through the mail he'd just picked up as he walked back to the house. One item was a large flat envelope. He opened it and smiled. The certificate for Cadie's AKC certification.

Hope looked up as he rushed into the house.

"Honey! It came in! Four weeks after we passed that test, doing it their way, her certificate has finally come."

The familiar *click-click-click* of toenails on the floor announced Cadie coming in to see what all the excitement was about. He held the certificate out for her to see. "Look, girl! You did it! Are you ready for a surprise?"

She didn't read it, of course, but did seem to think it had an intriguing odor, probably provided by the animals the sender had touched before putting her certificate in the envelope. But she was spending more time with it than David thought it would take to just smell it.

He went to his desk and pulled out a green therapy-dog vest with her badge on it. "See, girl? I've already got it for you."

He slipped the vest on the dog. She didn't object at all. It almost looked as if she were smiling.

"Honey, get the camera. By the way, where's Shelby? I want a picture of the two of them together."

"She's over at Sophie's house. She'll be back after dinner."

"Well, let me get a picture of the two of you." He held out his hand for the camera.

"No, let me take it. You're her handler. You should be in the picture." She snapped the picture, then the phone rang, and she answered it. "Hello."

A moment later, she quickly reached for a notepad and pencil, and sat down. "Okay, calm down, calm down. Tell me exactly what happened."

She listened, nodding. "Okay ... uh huh ... lost how many teeth?" Another pause, then, "Okay. The first thing you want to do is put those in milk."

The voice on the phone rose to be audible to David, although he couldn't make out the words.

"Yes, I'm serious," Hope said. "Put them in milk. Now, you need to go to the nearest emergency room. What's the closest hospital to your house? Okay, perfect." She made a note of the answer on her pad. "I'll meet you there in about twenty minutes. Yes, it's going to be all right."

She hung up the phone and turned to David. "I've got an emergency. A three-year-old just knocked out his front teeth. Call Sophie's parents and ask them if Shelby can stay there until we come get her, okay? I have to grab my bag." With that, she disappeared upstairs.

"Sure," David said to an empty room.

He barely had time to make the call before Hope came back downstairs and rushed through the house. She stopped at the door. "Aren't you coming?"

"Me?"

"No. Cadie. But you're her handler, so you have to go too. She's a therapy dog. Time to prove all those journals right."

"Uh, she's a therapy dog all right, but she's never been in a hospital."

"I keep telling you God's timing is perfect. C'mon. It's time to move. Let's go!"

Hope exited the house, leaving David talking to himself.

"They're your hospital privileges, not mine," he called after her. Turning to Cadie, he said, "C'mon girl, time to go to work."

An emergency room is usually a zoo: Phones ringing, machines hissing and beeping, people shouting orders and bustling around. It's all controlled pandemonium. David had a moment of panic. How would Cadie handle all this, with no preparation? Perhaps a better question would be, How would everyone else handle Cadie?

The noise died down almost immediately as everyone stared at the sight of a German shepherd walking through the ER waiting room. Hope strode through the doors to the patient area, flashing her ID to the security guard. David and Cadie were fast on her heels as the guard tried to block

David's way, but he politely slid past him, saying only, "I'm with her." The guard didn't challenge Cadie.

Even before they went through the double doors to the treatment area, they could hear the screaming of a child. The noise was almost deafening as they pushed through the doors.

Heads swiveled in disbelief toward Cadie as they moved into the heart of the emergency room. Before anyone overcame the shock and could object, the screaming stopped. Cadie had moved to the child's side and began to nuzzle against him. The little boy responded by putting his left arm around her.

Hope knelt in front of the child, took the towel away, and saw a bloody mess. She was able to stabilize the boy and patch him up until the formal work could be done in the office on Monday. Through the entire ordeal, the boy never let go of Cadie, and, amid all the tubes and wires of an ER environment, she made no effort to move. The youngster did not cry or scream again. The parents were both astonished and grateful, and the staff were as well—if not a bit dumbfounded at what they'd just witnessed.

When they were finished, David looked with intense pride at his two girls. "Good job, ladies. I'm so proud of you both." He ruffled Cadie's fur. "Finally, girl, we're able to make a difference and serve someone."

And it wouldn't be the last time, as the journey was only just beginning.

FIFTEEN

SHORTLY AFTER THE incident in the ER, David responded to a call from the director of the Children's Museum, asking for help with their story time. They needed a well-behaved German shepherd to help tell a story to a group of young readers. He was delighted to have the chance, and soon he and Cadie were at the museum, meeting the director at the door.

"Thank you for being able to join us on such short notice. I'm really sorry for that, but I'm glad you're here. I'd like to introduce you to Officer Peter Jackson."

The policeman smiled. "Hi. How ya doin'?"

"Great. Glad to be here. How can we help?"

"Well, the department won't let us bring our K-9s, because they frown on having police dogs in with a lot of small children in a confined space. City rules prevent us from taking our dogs out on nonpolice business, so we had to leave the working dogs at the station. Glad they were able to find somebody to bring in a pet."

"Cadie is more than a pet. She's an animal-assistance therapy dog. She's a highly trained working dog too, just a different type."

"Sure, she is."

Sensing the tension, the director interjected, "We're about to begin story time. If you gentlemen could follow me, please."

They followed him into the reading center. David stopped the officer just before they opened the door. "Here, take her lead. Keep her on the left. You'll know what to do. I'll be giving her signals from the back of the room, so you won't have any problems."

The officer looked surprised, then frowned, as if a bit annoyed. As a K-9 officer, he probably objected to being told how to handle a dog. But when the doors opened, his annoyance was instantly replaced by a smile as they walked into the room and onto the stage. David headed to the back of the room. Cadie followed the officer on lead.

"Boys and girls," the director said, smiling, "this is Officer Pete and Cadie. They have a wonderful story to share with you." He handed the book to the officer.

"Hi, boys and girls. Cadie and I would like to tell you the story of Officer Mike and Buck the Safety Dog. Just like in the story, I'm here to talk to you about safety. So, let's see what Officer Mike and Buck have to say."

As the officer sat, so did Cadie. He never saw David give a signal to Cadie. The officer began to read, and David gave a signal for Cadie to lie down. She complied but remained in a very alert position, watching the kids. As the officer read the story and they learned about Buck, the dog in the book, David silently had Cadie do some of the similar antics that Buck was doing in the story. The kids were enthralled and fascinated watching her, often laughing and clapping their hands as the dog appeared to be acting out what the officer was reading. Fortunately, Officer Pete was up to the task of being upstaged by a dog. But he was clearly surprised at how well Cadie acted without, at least from his perspective, being given a single command.

Afterward, the center director told David, "That dog is amazing. You have a very special dog on your hands. Look at the impact she's having on these kids."

"Yes, I agree; she is very special."

"It's more than that. She's really unique. Look at how the kids are paying attention to her. Have you ever heard of canine reading?"

"It may look like she understands the book that's being read, but I assure you she doesn't even know how to write, much less read."

"Actually, what I'm talking about is a program where therapy dogs are used to help disadvantaged kids learn how to read. You might want to check that out. I'll get you some information on the program before you leave."

The director left to get the material, while David closely observed the kids.

After they left the museum, David put Cadie in the car, looked at his watch, then pulled out his cell phone and called Hope's office. "Hi, Debbie. It's David. Is Dr. Hyler still at lunch? Great. Can I talk to her? Thanks."

"Hello?"

"Hi, honey. Have you come across anything in your journals about canine reading programs?"

"Are you planning to teach her to read now?"

"Ha, ha. Been there with that joke. It's where you use a therapy dog to work with disadvantaged kids to help them learn how to read."

"Really? Therapy dogs can do that?"

"I just saw it. Cadie did it here at the museum, without even being trained for it."

"That's terrific. But to answer your question, I haven't seen anything, and I don't even know where I'd start to look. What are you thinking?"

"I was thinking I could contact Shelby's school, and see what happens."

The following morning, David walked into the office of the school principal, Dr. Milford, to follow through on the idea.

"I've been doing some reading about this," Dr. Milford said enthusiastically. "It's where a therapy dog is used to work with children who are having a hard time learning to read. Typically, these kids have trouble because of a lack of confidence, poor support at home, and large classrooms that prevent teachers from providing as much one-on-one assistance as they'd like. Since the dogs are nonjudgmental and nonthreatening, the process pulls these kids out of their shells and helps them become part of the normal classroom environment. I'm certainly open to trying it here."

"I hadn't heard about it before yesterday," David said, "when I saw it in action. My own dog did it without even being trained for it."

"Amazing. Bring her in, and let's see how it works."

A few weeks later, David and Cadie were at the school as part of a pilot test program. David sat off to the side, smiling and watching as Cadie listened to the young child read. The school library was quiet, and as the child read something incorrectly, David would give a signal, and Cadie would put her paw up on the book.

"Great job," David said. "Cadie loved how you read that, and she wants to hear it again. Would you read that again to her?"

The child smiled and read with more confidence: "Rover took the ball and went 'outsid' to play."

"Wow! I've never seen her want to hear a line three times, but she's kept her paw on that spot. I think she wants to hear it again. Are you ready?"

The youngster nodded. "Rover took the ball and went outside to play."

Cadie removed her paw as David praised the child. "Perfect!"

They finished the book, and David put it away. The child and Cadie got up, and he took Cadie's leash. With David's help, they walked down the hall to the classroom.

As he turned to go to another classroom for his next student, David noticed a small child and her friend off to the side. The youngster seemed to be trying to blend into the wall, anxiety on her face. He immediately knew the child was afraid of Cadie. He approached slowly and put Cadie in the down position, where he could speak quietly to the youngster. "Hi there. What's the matter?"

Her friend answered for her. "She's afraid of dogs."

"Oh really? Well, Cadie is not really a dog. She's a little girl too, a very special little girl. I'll tell you what. Why don't you come and touch the tip of her tail? You don't have to get anywhere near her mouth, just touch her tail."

Both girls came over shyly to touch the dog's tail.

"Wow! Cadie really liked that. I'll tell you what. If you rubbed her back, I bet you could put her to sleep and let her take a nap right here in the hallway. Would you like to try that?"

The little girl nodded but still said nothing. She began to gently rub the dog's back. David gave Cadie a signal to lie down all the way and feign sleep.

"You can touch her ear if you want. It's really soft. You won't feel anything like it anywhere else."

The little girl touched the ear and smiled. The two friends got back to their feet. Her friend said, "We'd better be getting back to class."

"All right. Good-bye, girls. I'll see you later. Any time you want to say hi to Cadie, just let me know."

The girls walked back to class, casting several glances over their shoulders. Cadie did not move until he gave her the command to get back up.

"You're doing some amazing work here," a voice said.

David looked back to see Dr. Milford behind him. "Thank you."

"I'm astonished. That dog is incredibly special. More people need to know about this." Dr. Milford paused, as if lost in thought. "In fact, I believe I know just how to make that happen." He moved swiftly down the hall, giving all appearances of someone on a mission.

David scratched behind Cadie's ears. "It's good to be recognized, isn't it, girl?"

It had been several weeks since Dr. Milford had that flash of insight in the hallway. But, true to his word, he followed through with an idea. Now, Cadie lay on the couch in the living room as the family waited for the news to come on TV.

"This is so exciting," Hope said. "I'm so proud of you and Cadie."

"Dr. Milford surprised me by setting up this interview."

"There you are," Shelby said. "You look good, Daddy. Aw-w-w, look at Cadie."

David put a finger to his lips. "Shh. This is my debut."

The face of a news reporter came on the TV. A young woman, professionally attired and full of energy, she started right into the story. "Good evening, ladies and gentleman. Have I got a story for you! With me here today are David Hyler and his German shepherd, Cadie, and she's no ordinary dog. She's a dog who was rescued from horrible abuse and now helps rescue children from the prison of illiteracy by teaching kids to read. That's right; you heard me. A dog teaches kids to read. David, tell us about it."

She held out the microphone, and David said, "Children get to practice their reading skills by reading to Cadie. This one-on-one environment removes much of the stress involved in a classroom full of other children."

The reporter added, "Since this program was started, we have been told that these students have not only learned to read but also caught up with their peers in less than eight weeks. This is Wendy Delvano reporting for—"

David switched off the set. "Wow! ... that came out better than I thought! Maybe I should give some thought to doing something more with Cadie. What do you think about getting her involved at church with teaching kids to read the Bible?"

"That's a great idea," Hope said. "Why don't you check with the church? I bet Pastor Fordham would love something like that!"

"I will. I'll do it tomorrow. I'll touch base with him and see what opportunities there are. In fact, vacation Bible school might be just the ticket."

SIXTEEN

DAVID PITCHED HIS proposal to Pastor Fordham the following morning. Nodding with apparent understanding and offering a slight smile from time to time, Fordham took it all in. David, buoyed by the growing confidence in his pastor's affirmation, concluded by saying, "So, what do you think?"

The pastor shook his head. "Absolutely not."

Taken aback, David asked, "What do you mean, sir?"

Fordham, a big man with a strong ego that often bordered on being overbearing, kept pushing his dark-framed glasses up the bridge of his nose. "I simply will not allow a filthy animal in the house of the Lord."

David couldn't hide his offense at the comment. His voice rose slightly. "What do you mean by 'filthy'? She's certified to be in hospitals and doctor's offices, and she has been in schools and anywhere else any human is allowed to be."

"But not in my church. David, I had a dog once that dug holes in the yard. I put too much time and effort into my yard, and I couldn't allow that. So, I took the stupid animal to the pound."

"You do realize that dog was probably put down, don't you?"

"Not my problem. The dog was messing up my yard. She wasn't my responsibility. You see, David, animals do not have an eternal soul. They are meant to be used by us for whatever purpose we see fit, but we don't use them to proclaim the Word of God. You are ascribing a worth to this animal that it doesn't deserve. These animals are worthless."

This was the last thing David expected to hear after relaying the story of everything Cadie had done and been through. The anger surged in him, the need to defend her strong within him, but he continued to tamp it down. "This dog has helped dozens of people—"

Fordham interrupted. "I don't care. You're not hearing me."

"Oh, I'm hearing you all right. I just can't believe what I'm hearing."

The pastor put an end to the conversation by standing. "Our meeting is done today. Thank you for coming in. I would strongly advise you to reconsider the path you're on before you find yourself on a journey with a destination you're not going to like. Now, if you will excuse me, I have work to do."

David turned and walked slowly out of the office. Rejected. Unwanted. Again.

Back at the school, as they walked to another classroom for a student, David told Cadie, "You know, for two people considered to be worthless by the church, we seem to be doing a pretty good job helping folks. I don't think our pastor is right, do you? I mean, isn't service to one another in His name one of the key acts Christ calls us to perform? What do you think, girl?"

A voice behind them said, "You're David Hyler, aren't you?"

He turned to see a young mother behind him. "Yes, ma'am."

"I want to thank you for helping my daughter overcome her fear and learn to read."

David smiled but was confused. "I'm not sure I follow you. I know all the parents in our reading program, but I don't recognize you."

"I didn't mean in your program. Cadie helped my daughter overcome her fear of dogs, but we didn't know that. You see, my husband and I kept hearing our daughter talking to somebody at night after we tucked her into bed. It happened again the other night, so we poked our heads in the door, and there she was, sitting underneath the covers of her bed, reading her book by flashlight."

"I still don't see what—"

"She was terrified of dogs until she met Cadie. Only now, when we looked in, she had one of her stuffed animals under the cover with her— one she has renamed Cadie—and she was reading to it."

"Really?"

"Now Cadie is all she talks about. Every night, she's been reading, and it's all because you took a few minutes to spend time with her in the hallway one day and help her through her fear. I just wanted to say, 'God bless you, and God bless Cadie.' It's too bad there aren't more like you."

"Thank you. Just hearing that we've helped is a huge reward for our efforts." David watched them walk away. "No doubt in my mind," he muttered. "The pastor *is* wrong."

He turned to continue down the hallway just as the principal came out of the office and called to him. "David? Got a minute?"

"For you? Always. What can I do for you, Dr. Milford?"

The principal indicated a severe-looking man in a dark suit, standing and reading something, and said, "This is Mr. Crane, the Superintendent of Schools for our county."

"David," the man said, "it's certainly nice to finally meet you. You don't mind if I call you David, do you?"

"Of course not."

"I've certainly heard a lot about you."

The principal said, "David, you have been of great benefit to the school, and I want you to know—"

"Dr. Milford," the superintendent cut in, "would you mind terribly if David and I had a word together?"

The principal did not move. The superintendent put his hand on the principal's shoulder and added, "Alone, please?"

The principal seemed agitated as he got up. Before he left the room, he said, "David, you've done fantastic work here."

David, confused, stared at the principal's back as he left the room. When the principal had closed the door, the superintendent said, "Are you a religious man, David?"

David's attention was immediately drawn back to the man before him. "I don't understand. What does that have to do with anything, Mr. Crane?"

"I was playing golf the other day with a very good friend of mine. I believe you know him." He looked up from what he'd been reading. "John Fordham, Pastor John Fordham." He focused his attention back on the awards and pictures on the principal's walls. "He was telling me about some vacation bible school you're running."

David could not imagine where this was heading. "I'm not running a vacation bible school. I did offer Cadie's assistance at the one the church is running, but that's not happening. Besides, what does that have to do with the reading program?"

"I don't have to tell you what the possibilities for controversy are if word got out that we were mixing Christian education with public education." Now he faced David directly. "Do I?"

Frustration building, David began to raise his voice ever so slightly. "I told you, my involvement with the vacation bible school is not going to happen."

"I know. John explained it all to me. The problem is, your little project is starting to get media attention, and the possibility of you being connected with a church program ... well, I just can't explain to you what a hornet's nest that would open up."

"My only intent within this school is to help kids who have difficulty reading, and Cadie and I have done just that." This was going nowhere, as far as David was concerned. Even Cadie sensed the confusion as she observed the two men going back and forth like players in a tennis match.

"Yes, I know. I've seen the piece on television." He rewarded David with an insincere smile. "Fine piece. You're doing admirable work, but I find myself having to look at a bigger picture."

"And teaching students to read doesn't fit into the big picture?"

"David, I oversee sixty-five schools, fifteen hundred teachers—teachers who are in difficult contract negotiations as we speak—and thirty-five thousand students. How is it going to look if one little old school in that program has more success teaching students how to read using a dog instead of trained professionals?"

So that was it. He and Cadie embarrassed the administration and wounded their egos. "Fine. I won't do any more interviews."

"No, that's not enough."

Exasperated, David asked, "What more do you want from me?"

The superintendent steepled his fingers. "The impact you are having on that little group of underachievers is just not worth it in the grand scheme of things. The K-9 reading program is canceled."

"What?"

"Effective immediately."

David's mouth fell open. "You can't be serious."

"Oh, I can. And I am. And I'm sure, once you get yourself calmed down, that you are going to understand."

David got up and grabbed a piece of paper as he headed for the door. His anger finally reaching the boiling point, he said, "No, I don't. And I won't. Maybe it'll help if you write it down, and I can have one of Cadie's students read it to me." Punctuating that last statement, David threw the paper down on the desk in front of the superintendent and stormed out of the office.

The superintendent smiled a crooked little grin, eminently satisfied that he had so easily accomplished his mission. He called through the door, "Dr. Milford, you can have your office back. I believe we are done here."

Hope was in the kitchen when David and Cadie got home from school. She smiled brightly but didn't look up, as she was focused on preparing the evening meal on the hot stove. "Hi, honey. Guess what we're having for dinner?"

David simply walked on into the living room and plopped down on the couch, as if he were exhausted. Cadie headed over to her safe spot and lay down where she could keep an eye on him.

Concerned by Cadie's reaction more than anything else, Hope followed David, wiping her hands on a kitchen towel.

"What's wrong, sweetheart?"

"I don't want to talk about it."

Hope's concern turned to hurt. She glanced back over at Cadie. The attitude of the dog and the way she was watching David was not lost on her. She went back to the kitchen to work on the meal but periodically glanced back in at David.

He simply sat with his head down.

"Well," she called out, trying to cheer him up, "how about if I change the subject? Do you remember that job offer I received?"

"The one in New England?" David sounded less than interested.

"Yes, that's the one."

"Why do you ask?"

She could tell, at that moment, he didn't really care. He was just going through the motions of a conversation.

She walked back into the living room. "Well," she said with excitement, "they called again. They made me an offer. They are very eager for me to come and meet the whole family."

"You do realize it would involve a lot of change, especially selling the practice?"

"I know, sweetheart, but it's a great opportunity for me, and you can do your software work from anywhere. Besides, we'll get through the changes together. After all, God is on our side."

He shrugged, his voice still flat. "Why not? There's no reason to stay here anymore. No one cares about some guy and his dog."

Now Hope knew something had happened. She'd seen that look before, heard that tone. David had just lost something very valuable. But she also knew that he'd eventually share the burden with her. She simply had to wait for his timing. Even Cadie was smart enough to leave David alone. That said a lot.

As she returned to the kitchen to finish making dinner, she pondered, *Maybe I can learn from Cadie … just as David seems to be doing.*

SEVENTEEN

MOVING IS ONE of the top "life events" that contribute to stress. It doesn't matter if you move across town or across the country, moving is a major source of stress. Of course, moving was not new to David. The military had moved him all over the country. Before that were all the moves growing up. So, to him, moving was uneventful. It was part of life. Don't get too attached to anyone or anything, and then it doesn't hurt when you leave. Move on.

Not so with Shelby. She experienced a set of challenges and emotions David didn't recall ever having experienced in his life. Of course, truth be told, he'd simply pushed them aside and tried to forget them. Fortunately, somewhere along the way, he'd learned that was a really bad approach. Even so, he remained totally unprepared to help Shelby work through the pain of leaving her friends behind, much less coping with all the anxieties of being in a new home and school. Fortunately for both of them, they had Hope. Here, she rose to the challenge of helping everyone, herself included, look forward in anticipation, not backward in regret, when facing the challenges God was placing before them. Challenges, as she told them, that were, in fact, blessings.

As life began to settle into a new rhythm, David sat in his new home office, unpacking. As he pulled out a picture of his grandfather, voices from his past began to play in his head.

He heard Margaret say, "I hope you're happy. You just ruined my retirement."

He heard G'anny say, "Your mommy is not coming back."

He heard his mother say, "I'll never leave you."

He heard his father say, "You're worthless."

The voices continued, telling him of Smokey's passing, then Pastor Fordham's comments, and, finally, the statements of the superintendent of schools. Trapped in the past, he felt paralyzed as the relentless voices dealt him blow after blow after blow. He was reeling.

It was then that he focused on the photo of his grandfather. Looking at the kind face of his grandfather, he finally heard some positive reinforcement in his head. He heard his grandfather say, "I love you." Then, he heard him say, "If you ever need anything, let me know." Well, he did need something. And he needed it now.

Pastor Fordham's condemnation of Cadie, and of David's desires to serve God, were never far from the forefront of his mind. No one else seemed to share the pastor's opinion, but David knew there would be others who didn't share his own vision. He could let them get him down again, or he could prepare a response. He just didn't know which he would do.

He opened another box to unpack it. On top of the box was the drawing he had done at G'anny's house and another picture of his grandfather. In his head, he heard his grandfather tell him not to dwell in the past, so that he could be prepared for the victories God had in store for him. He smiled at the picture, then continued digging through the packing paper, where he found his grandfather's Bible. His decision had been made—he would prepare a response.

"What was it you used to say, Grandpa?" he murmured.

"David?" Hope stood in the doorway. "Are you all right? You're awfully quiet in here."

David was frantically going through the pages of the Bible he'd just unpacked. He tried to assure Hope that he was okay, saying absently, "I'm fine."

"What are you doing?"

"Preparing for battle."

"Against whom?"

"Against being hurt, unloved, and unwanted. You've said it all along: Cadie and I are on a journey. It's time I looked at the road map and started following the directions. It's exactly the same as what Grandpa told me: 'A horse is prepared for the day of battle, but victory belongs to the Lord.'"

"So, you're saying—"

"Grandpa said the Lord would use me, but I had to be prepared for it to happen. I've been letting other people control what happens in my life all the time. I need a plan. I need to arm myself so that I'm ready when I get the chance to be used. It's time for a change."

The following months were spent putting the house in order, acclimating Shelby to her new school, and getting Hope settled in to her new job, free of the burdens of practice ownership. Finally, as she often said, she was happy being able to just be a dentist. Meanwhile, David continued to study the Bible and prepare to serve others. Before they knew it, the beautiful fall in New England gave way to the first snowfall and thoughts of the holidays.

Hope and Shelby scurried around the room, decorating for Christmas, putting presents in shoe boxes. These were no ordinary shoe boxes; these were boxes of hope and smiles destined for children in lands most people tried to ignore, like Somalia.

Looking out the window, Hope called over her shoulder, "I love New England. It's so beautiful here. Thanks for moving us up here, honey."

Gesturing toward the shoe boxes, Shelby said, "Daddy, tell me again why we are doing this?"

He smiled at her. "These children have nothing. It's a great way for us to give to those who don't have much. And Christmas *is* the time for giving. When I was at the orphanage, I remember that the local townspeople would do something like this for us. It made us feel special."

"Speaking of giving," Hope said, "maybe we should give Cadie a present. Maybe a companion."

David frowned. "I'm not sure that's a good idea."

"Why not? Didn't you say shepherds need companionship with other dogs?"

"Yes, it's a hallmark of the breed, but what I meant was that it's not a good idea right now."

"It's Christmas. What better time to give a puppy as a present?"

David couldn't help but think back to the puppy that had come to his house, only to leave again just as quickly when he didn't react the way his dad had wanted him to. "That's exactly my point. A lot of people feel that way. But that's why rescues become inundated with dogs of all ages, shapes, sizes, and breeds in January. After the glitter fades, they're left with more unwanted, unloved dogs than they can possibly handle. Most rescues won't even adopt out a dog during December."

"But I still think she needs a companion."

"You're right; she does. Just not now. After the first of the year, I'll check out the rescue and see what they have. Fair enough?"

"Fair enough. Now let's go drop these presents off."

They were lucky to find the website for the LifeCare Center in Attleboro. There was no other drop-off point anywhere else close by.

David read from their brochure: "'LifeCare's nursing-home residents enjoy a homelike environment, inpatient rehabilitation therapy, and comfortable surroundings.'" He then added, "There are quite a few of these facilities around the country, but this one is in the vicinity. For our purpose, they work with Operation Christmas Child. The brochure says that last year, LifeCare alone filled almost a quarter-million shoe boxes with small toys, hard candy, school supplies, and hygiene items destined to go to small children in a wide range of places." He looked up at Hope. "That sounds like just what we're looking for."

"Yes, it does … let's go!"

As they drove, David looked over at Shelby. "You know, I always feel great when I can give something back. It's something Cadie taught me, and the more I follow her lead, the more I come to understand."

"I like that, Daddy. I want to follow her lead too."

"That's what we're doing."

David pulled into the driveway and parked. "I'll be right back," he said.

"Can I go with you?" asked Shelby.

"Of course!"

He helped her out of the car and gave her some of the decorated shoe boxes to carry.

Approaching the front desk, David asked, "Where do we take these?"

"Right over there," the receptionist said, smiling as she pointed to a stack of decorated shoe boxes like theirs. It looked as if it might be a staging area for Santa Claus!

They stacked their boxes neatly on a large pile of similar boxes.

"Thank you very much!" the receptionist said.

David and Shelby smiled, and then, hand in hand, returned to the car.

As he opened the car door for Shelby, Hope said, "Did you ask them about needing a therapy dog?"

"No. Was I supposed to?"

"You're the one who wants to serve," she said with a look that telegraphed, *You know you're missing the obvious; don't make me say it.*

"Yeah, right. Okay, be right back." He got Cadie out of the car and went back into the center and up to the receptionist.

She smiled again. "May I help you?"

"Hi, it's me again. Who would I speak to about perhaps using a service dog?"

"You mean one of the patients needing a service dog? I'm not sure I understand what you are talking about."

"I mean helping here with a therapy dog."

"Oh, wait a minute." She punched a button on the intercom and spoke into it. "Randi to the front lobby. Randi to the front lobby, please."

Pointing to a spacious sitting area with a crackling fire in a massive stone fireplace, she said, "You can have a seat over there. She'll be here in just a moment."

As promised, a few moments later, a woman approached and held out her hand. "Hi, I'm Randi. So, you want to bring in your pet?"

"Actually, she's a therapy dog."

"We already have one of those that comes in and does room visits."

"That's a start, but I was kind of thinking she could help out in other ways."

"I guess we could see about it. Can you be here on Tuesday at 10:00 a.m.?"

"Sure."

"All right, be here on Tuesday, and we'll see what we can work out for you. Merry Christmas."

"Merry Christmas to you too. And thank you."

"In the meantime, while you're here, let me show you around."

As David received a guided tour of LifeCare's rehabilitation unit, he noticed that the mood of many of the residents was similar to that of the weather outside. The expressions were reflective of the graying skies and dormant forests. One of the patients, Mary, sat staring at the floor. Like the forests surrounding the center she, too, looked lifeless. But inside, where no one could see, there was a life waiting to be reborn.

David learned that Mary had suffered back-to-back bouts of pneumonia, which left her gasping for breath every time she simply tried to sit up. A once-vibrant woman, she had been left a weakened, shadowy reflection of her former self. Now, she found herself a patient in a facility she never imagined she'd be a part of.

The latter revelation caught David by surprise because his tour had focused on the outpatient rehabilitation unit. Even though Mary had a home, she was also a resident of the nursing home, with no idea how long she might be here.

When he asked her, all she said was, "Until I get better."

According to the staff, that was expected to be quite a while. On good days, her progress was slow. On bad days, there was none at all. And Mary hadn't had a lot of good days. He quickly discovered she was expected to be there at least through the winter. They confided in him that they all hoped she could begin thinking of going home in the spring, but these days, no one talked of that.

To reach that goal, her therapist had a very specific plan for her to follow. That plan required her to walk—and to do it every day, which was something she didn't like to do anymore. She tired easily. She struggled to walk just a few feet. And when she did, she sat down exhausted, gasping for breath.

Randi shared more insights. "Most days, when she isn't trying to walk, Mary sits in her wheelchair and thinks about better times—times when she could walk on her own, times she used to spend with one (or all three) of her dogs, and times when she was free to be herself." Randi paused for a moment and then added, "But those times are all in the past."

In the present, like today, David imagined Mary felt like she was a prisoner.

As they walked in, David noticed Mary surveying the room. He couldn't imagine that she would see anything different, much less remarkable. He saw her gaze return to the floor. Winter had set in. Her future, as far as he could tell, resembled the landscape: bleak and uninviting. What reason would she have to go on?

Randi seemed to sense his thoughts, and commented, "Why don't we see if we can change her outlook on life?"

On Tuesday morning, at 10:00 a.m., David and Cadie walking in the door of the facility, about to embark on a journey neither of them could have imagined.

Randi walked up to Mary and said, "Mary ... I want you to meet someone."

No response.

"This is Cadie," Randi continued. "She's a therapy dog. Do you want to pet Cadie?"

David always got a kick out of how they never introduced him—only his dog! And that was okay with him. Cadie was the real star. So, it wasn't unusual to meet people, wherever he went, who said, "I know Cadie, but I don't know who you are. I see you here with her all the time, but ... uh ... what's your name, and what is it you actually do?" David loved it. He got to stay small and make God big!

In Mary's case, there was only the briefest of pauses before she looked up, rubbed Cadie's head, and stroked her ears. Mary was rewarded with a beautiful smile and a gentle nudge, as if to say, "More, more! That feels so-o-o-o-o good!"

Cadie got more. She knew how to melt a heart … no matter how cold or broken it might be.

Mary seemed almost mesmerized by Cadie. David could see it in her eyes. That *click* or *connection* was undeniable. And Cadie seemed to know it too. Oblivious to the surroundings, Mary was lost in the moment, focused totally on a dog that was happy simply being by her side. In fact, none of them had noticed Lisa, one of the physical therapists, quietly approach this unusual scene.

David watched, eyes misty, as time seemed to stand still. He could see the change in Mary, as if she were transported instantly to a better place and time. She seemed to be free again—free from the wheelchair and free in her spirit. Cadie had broken through the ice and helped Mary discover spring again in her heart.

The power of a therapy dog … wow! The power of God working through His creation. David was in awe.

In that instant, respectful of the moment, Lisa leaned over and quietly asked Mary if she would like to walk Cadie.

"Oh, yes!" came the immediate, enthusiastic reply. Her gaze never left Cadie as she began to smile. The ice was melting. God was warming this woman's heart.

With her walker positioned in front of her, the therapist behind her, and Cadie to her left, Mary decided it was time to walk. Buoyed by the emotions of the moment, she grasped her walker and stood with a sense of confidence that, unfortunately, didn't transfer to her uncertain and nearly forgotten legs. They gave way, and she began to fall—directly on Cadie!

As time stood still, one of David's worst fears as a handler was coming true right before his eyes. Cadie would either get hurt or cause an injury to someone else, or both. Mary's walker was no help; it was in front of her. The therapist tried to catch her but was on the wrong side.

David had to make a decision—let Cadie go, and catch Mary, hoping his dog wouldn't bolt; or protect his dog, and hope Mary would not get hurt in the fall. He decided to trust Cadie and try to prevent injury to

Mary. In doing that he violated rule number one and number two—never put your partner in jeopardy of getting hurt, and never release control of your dog.

As he released Cadie and caught Mary, the therapist was then able to move in and help Mary regain solid footing. They breathed a sigh of relief and looked around. Nobody seemed to even have noticed.

Instead, everyone was focused on Cadie.

David hadn't realized it, but, even though he had released her lead, signaling her that it was okay to move, Mary had placed her hand on the dog's back, using the animal to help catch her as well as to steady herself. And Cadie hadn't moved. Had she moved even a foot, she would have pulled Mary down over her walker and onto the floor, but Cadie didn't even flinch. Instead, she stood her ground, holding Mary up and ready to help ease her fall! This was simply unheard of. She wasn't trained to do anything like this.

The staff had seen therapy dogs before. And, without exception, each person commented to David that they'd never seen one so poised and so confident. In fact, the last therapy dog they'd had at the center had bolted under similar circumstances and created problems by knocking over equipment and two patients! But not this time, and not this dog.

In the brief instant of time that hangs between success and disaster, Cadie established her reputation at the center as an animal-assistance therapy dog without equal.

David was convinced, however, that Cadie didn't understand what all the fuss was about. She was simply being herself. She was waiting patiently to help. She was ready to walk with Mary for as long as needed. And she had shown she was also ready to do whatever else Mary needed. Now that she was on her feet and steady, she looked back and up at him as if to say, "Ready whenever you are!"

Apparently, Mary was ready. She took the walker with both hands, the lead in her left, and set off ... slowly at first, but each step built her confidence. Cadie paced herself with her walk and, every so often, would look back over her shoulder to check on the woman. Each time, she was rewarded with a smile from Mary. About a hundred feet later, Mary took a break. Only then did everyone realize she had walked four times farther than ever before!

At last, Mary sat back down in her wheelchair, smiling, out of breath, and petting Cadie.

David felt Mary had no need to escape to another place and time anymore. Not when Cadie was part of her reality. Perhaps there was some life left in the forest surrounding her after all.

By the time Hope got home that evening, David and Cadie were already there. He looked up as she came in, and said, "Hi, honey, how was your day?"

"Awesome! I saw lots of patients who really needed our services, and got to conduct my first lecture to the students. It's the type of day I've always wanted. How was your first day at LifeCare?"

"Incredible." David was beaming. "I've never seen anything like it. Cadie did great. I, on the other hand, broke the first two rules of being a responsible handler."

"Oh really? What did you do?"

"Well, rule number one is, never put your dog at risk. I put Cadie at risk. Rule number two is, never relinquish control of your dog, and I let go of her leash. In fact, I put it in the hands of a seventy-year-old woman who can't walk."

"Please tell me nothing happened," Hope said with genuine concern.

"Actually, something did happen." He paused. "More miracles." David launched into the story of what happened at the facility, becoming more and more animated.

"Wow!" Hope said. "It does sound like Cadie is still making miracles happen."

"I'm beginning to get the point," David said. "I really believe this is what God wants her to do."

"You think?"

"Yeah, I think."

"But, next time, sweetheart, tell me the story like Paul Harvey does, with the ending first. I can't stand the suspense!"

Hope must have noticed the answering machine blinking just then, for she walked toward it. "Have you had a chance to listen to these yet?"

"Not yet. Sorry."

Hope walked over and pressed the Play button. The first message began. "Attention, homeowners. Do you want to refinance?" She scowled and hit the Delete button. "I thought we were on the do-not-call list."

"We were, in North Carolina, but not here. It takes several weeks for the change to take place."

The second message was more interesting. "David, this is Angela from German Shepherd Rescue down in North Carolina. I got your message that you're looking for a companion for Cadie. We happen to have a male shepherd here that comes from a tough background like hers. If you are up for another challenge, we think Simba would be a good fit for you. Please give me a call back, and we can go over the details."

"That's great," Hope said.

"Hope he likes snow."

The third call was from a local youth pastor at their new church, Ocean State Baptist Church. "David, this is Michael St. Clair. I've heard about what you and your dog did down south, and I wonder if you could give me a call. I'll be available until 8:00 p.m."

"Oh great, another church wants to excommunicate us, and we're not even members yet."

She frowned. "Pastor Fordham's not up here. You need to let go of that."

"Sorry."

"There's only one way to find out. It's 7:50. Give this guy a call, and see what he wants."

David sighed and reluctantly agreed. "You're right. After such a good day, I should be able to stand up to another beating or two."

Hope rolled her eyes as she handed him the phone. "Put it on speaker, so I can hear."

Someone answered on the other end, and David said, "Pastor St. Clair, please. David Hyler calling."

The voice said, "Please call me Pastor Mike, David. Thanks for calling back. Welcome to Ocean State Baptist Church, by the way. We want to thank you for visiting with us."

"Thanks."

"I ran across an article about you and what you've done with your dog. I found it really interesting, so I did a little more digging and found a video online about the K-9 Reading Program you did down south."

David braced himself. *Here we go again. I thought I'd moved away from all this.*

Pastor Mike continued. "I want to tell you how incredible it is. In fact, I was wondering if you'd like to speak to our teen youth group and tell them how you're serving God with your dog. How would next Saturday at 10:00 a.m. work for you?"

David nearly dropped the phone, and his mouth fell open. *Huh?*

Hope batted her eyes, following up with a goofy grin, to communicate, *I told you so.*

Playfully, David stuck his tongue out at her.

Refocusing on the moment, he responded, "Me? Um … I'm not a preacher."

Pastor Mike laughed pleasantly. "You don't have to be a preacher. To reach these kids, you just have to be yourself, and let them see your heart for the Lord. Do that, and they'll get it. Just explain why you use Cadie and what makes her so special."

Hope tapped him lightly on the arm and whispered, "Do it!"

"Okay, count us in. We'll be there." He hung up.

Hope gave him a big hug and said, "That was such a lovely beating, my dear."

EIGHTEEN

S ATURDAY CAME, AND David found himself at Ocean State Baptist Church, standing nervously outside a large conference room with Pastor Mike. "We have about thirty high school and college kids in there," Mike said. "Are you ready to give them some motivation?"

David looked down at Cadie. "Well, sweetie, are you ready?"

Cadie stood alert, her smile matching her wagging tail, and her ears perked, ready to face whatever challenge might be ahead.

David glanced back at the youth-group leader. "She's ready—not so sure about me, though."

"You'll be fine. Do your best, and let God do the rest. I'll go in and introduce you; then you come out right after me," Pastor Mike said as he stepped out onto the stage.

David leaned down to whisper to Cadie, "All right, sweetheart, let's do this. Here's our debut for God as a ministry team. This is what we've been preparing for."

Pastor Mike gave a short introduction and concluded with, "So, right now, let me introduce you to David and Cadie. They are going to give you their unique perspective on how they share God's story. We're ready for you, pal."

David walked out to polite applause. Cadie took her place beside him. He looked out over the group. "When Pastor Mike asked me to speak to the youth group here at Ocean State, I was excited! After all, I've always wanted to be an actor, and to have a stage, a captive audience, well ... it doesn't get better than this."

He paused and then continued. "Then, reality set in. Hey, nobody's going to hand me a script. I gotta do this on my own! My excitement gave way to anxiety ... maybe even a little fear. I realized I'd have to come up with something to talk about. Then I remembered what Pastor Mike had said. 'Like a devotional,' or did he say, 'a lesson'? Maybe he meant a sermon? Hey, wait a minute! I haven't graduated from seminary. I've never even been to one. Me speak to a church youth group?"

David took a breath and smiled. "But bottom line: I'm it. You're stuck with me. And, like I said, I want to be an actor, and part of being one means telling a story. So, I asked myself, What kind of story can I tell here? What's my inspiration? Where can I find an example?"

He held up his hands. "And then, the light came on! Did you know that God is a great storyteller? Noted Christian author and speaker Tim Downs highlights storytelling as one of the key attributes of God. And I agree with him."

David moved around the side of the podium to get closer to his audience.

"Do you agree?" David asked. "Think about it for a minute; I think you'll agree, if you don't already. For any skeptics out there, let me challenge you to look for those stories yourself. You can find a collection of our Lord's greatest stories in the Bible. In fact, the Bible is much more than just basic instructions for life; it's full of stories of all kinds. Some are very simple ... others, epic in scale.

"Regardless of size, the fact is, stories are such an integral part of the Bible that, if you look closely, you'll see that Jesus always included at least one parable, or story, to illustrate His point every time He taught. Put another way, He never taught without telling a story.

"Why do you suppose that is? It's because a story has a way of becoming a part of you like no other form of communication can. Stories allow us to dream and experience things we can't find any other way. We lower our defenses, to listen and even participate, so, before we know it, we're involved! And you know what else? You *remember* stories!

"I'm not as good a storyteller as God. Not even close. But Genesis 1:27 says: 'So God created man in his own image, in the image of God he created him; male and female he created them.' Did you catch that? I'm created in His image. I share His attributes. That means I can be a storyteller too. So, I'd like to tell you a story of my own. I'll warn you now: I need help. That means you need to participate. So, close your eyes if you want, but no sleeping; listen to the words, and put yourself in the story. Try to become the character you're about to meet. Imagine for the next few minutes that I'm talking about *you*. Ready? Okay, let's go."

David moved back to the podium and began to paint a picture for them, using words. He didn't simply tell them about Cadie's experience in captivity; he described it in a way that made it come to life. He wanted them to be there. He wanted them to see it. He wanted them to know what she had been through.

He looked up from the notes and said, "Can you relate to what I'm saying? Have you ever been hurt by someone you cared about? Have you ever been praised one minute and beaten down the next? Have you ever been hugged, only to be hit or yelled at when all you wanted was another hug? Have you ever wondered if you were loved? Have you ever felt lost, forgotten, worthless? Have you ever given up hope for a future? If you can answer yes to any of these questions, then you can identify, at least in part, with my friend in the story. And it's easier to tell the story easier if your audience can identify with your character."

After he finished painting his picture, he surveyed the young faces to see if he was reaching them. Clearly, he had, if their tears were any indication. These kids got it!

"Are you searching for a way to serve? Wondering what you can do for God? Sometimes it takes a helper, a friend, to come alongside and encourage you. Or maybe you can be that encourager for someone else. Either way, we all have a calling. My encourager was a German shepherd named Cadie." He gestured to the dog who had been sitting quietly by his side the whole time.

"Ladies and gentlemen, we have a commission from God to tell the unsaved world the greatest story ever written. It's the most serious task we'll ever have, and we need to take it seriously.

"Sounds like a daunting task, doesn't it? To be a storyteller to the world! Wow! *Daunting* doesn't even begin to describe it. Try *overwhelming*. I mean, how do you tell God's story to the world? But, just as Paul had Barnabas, and each of the early missionaries had a partner, each of you needs a partner to help you meet your calling in the Lord. Ask God what He thinks. And then, be prepared to accept the answer God sends you— regardless of what it is or how He sends it!

"In my case, He sent a dog no one else wanted; that was His way of helping me tell the story of how love can transform lives. It's a story of rescue, redemption, and service. Together, Cadie and I explain how He did this for us, just as we do it for others. But the key is that I wouldn't be able to do this if people didn't ask me about her first. You see, I can't go up to people and ask if they know their destiny when they die. But I can talk about my dog. And God knew that. So, my angel in a fur coat opens doors to allow me to share His story.

"I challenge you to live for Christ. Share stories about Christ. The more people hear and see examples from your own life, the greater your testimony. Never assume you have to fit into a cookie-cutter mold of evangelism. God has given each of us gifts. Use the gifts He's given you! Be creative. He is, so why shouldn't you be too? Look at Cadie. Who would have thought a dog could help witness? But I would say to you, Why not? She's part of His creation too. Psalm 8:6 says, 'He put everything under our feet.' So, don't overlook the opportunities out there to help you share Christ!

"Sharing the gospel is telling the greatest story ever written! We're called to do it. So, be a storyteller. And, if you're like me and need help, ask God for a partner who will help you. But *tell* the story! Be like God. Be a storyteller!"

While David was talking, Pastor Mike slipped out down the hallway to find Randy Ward. Randy was the vice president of Boston Baptist College, a member of the church, and actively involved in teaching there as well. As David would soon learn, Mike and Randy were kindred spirits when it came to finding a way to share the gospel.

"Randy, you got a minute? You need to hear this guy talking to your youth group. I think he'd make a great guest speaker for your senior class up at the college."

"For which series? Missions?"

"Just go listen to him, and decide for yourself."

The two walked back down the hallway and slipped into the rear of the darkened auditorium.

As they listened to David talk and watched the reaction of the audience, Randy said, "The kids are really into this."

Mike nodded. "And it isn't easy to hold the attention of kids this age."

"Exactly what I was thinking. You're right. This is what we've been talking about as 'creative evangelism.' I think I need to invite this guy up to Boston."

Two weeks later, David and Cadie found themselves on the campus of a small Christian college in Boston, Massachusetts, about to speak to a group of seniors on a topic David couldn't have imagined a few short months earlier. As he began to have doubts and second thoughts about all this, Randy approached them in the parking lot. He greeted them warmly.

"Thanks for taking the time to come up here and talk with us."

"My pleasure."

Randy led them to the auditorium. "In this day and age, it's more critical than ever to get the message of the gospel out. It takes creativity to get people to pay attention. That's one of the aspects of your ministry that I love."

"Ministry?" David laughed. "I don't have a ministry."

"Oh, but you do! And you don't realize it." Randy grinned. "That's the beauty of it."

Willing to go along without really understanding, David offered a tongue-in-cheek reply. "Okay, then. I've got my shepherd; where's the flock?"

"Follow me." Randy smiled.

They walked into the lecture hall, and Randy gave a brief introduction. "We've been talking about creative evangelism. Today, we have David and Cadie here with us to give us an unusual perspective on sharing God's Word."

David walked to the front of the class amid the students' applause. "What I'm going to share with you is the story of a dog and the story of love. You see, Cadie taught me about love. We often work in hospitals and nursing homes, and Cadie has this ability to always go to the person who needs her the most. She just knows. For example, let me tell you what happened the other day."

NINETEEN

*S*MOKEY WAS ONE of a kind, irreplaceable. At least that was what David thought. But then, along came Cadie, a miracle. Not a replacement, but unique in her own right. Now he was thinking of a companion for her. Could lightning strike three times? Certainly, the story could not repeat itself.

And then, David met Simba, a two-tone brown male. He listened to the story of the animal at the rescue shelter, and his heart went out to the dog. At barely a year old, he had suffered terrible abuse. His owner then tried to neuter him with garden shears. David could not believe what he was hearing ... *garden shears?*

The man mutilated Simba and, in the process, nicked the femoral artery. As the dog tried to escape from his attacker, he left a trail of blood through the neighborhood, fatally bleeding. It was this trail, and the howls of a dog in pain, that led police to the man, still chasing him with the shears, still trying to complete the job. The man was arrested, and Simba was rushed to emergency medical treatment.

David shook his head as he read the account. How could a human being act this way? What was it in a person that would allow him to treat one of God's creations in this manner? The record didn't contain the punishment the man received, but David was sure that no matter what it was, it could never fit the crime.

He read on. After several weeks and two surgeries, Simba was able to be adopted out, and by the same police officer who was involved in his rescue. David frowned. What? That should be the end of the report. Why was there more?

The officer wanted to turn Simba into a K-9 police dog! *What an idiot,* David thought. *You don't do something like that with a dog of unknown lines.* Strike one. *And you certainly don't do it if you're not even a K-9 officer.* Strike two. Talk about not being qualified! Apparently, this officer used such brutal training methods that Simba developed a resistance to being trained, period.

The officer's supervisor found out and gave him a choice: the dog or his badge. Simba was returned to the shelter and later brought into the same rescue that had taken in Cadie. But his strong personality, massive strength, size of 110 pounds, and unpredictable behavior made adoption impossible. Like Cadie, he was now classified as "unadoptable."

"Another unwanted dog," David said. "Can I meet him?"

"I thought you might feel that way," the worker said.

David went out into the yard. There, he saw a beautiful animal, confident but relaxed. Simba regarded him with a look that David recognized as playful, maybe with a little potential mischief mixed in. He spent some time with the dog and was sure he would work out. However, there was one big hurdle to clear first.

He went to the car and brought Cadie back on a leash.

This was the big test: she had to accept him, or it was no-go.

As he approached with Cadie, the moment came. Like lightning, Simba lunged at Cadie. David reacted without thinking, and freed Cadie. He would be better able to protect her if he was free to move. But she didn't need help. She was smaller by twenty-five pounds, but size didn't matter. She held her ground—confident, poised, and ready.

Simba's teeth were huge. Everything about him was huge. His fur standing up made him look even more intimidating. As he lunged, Cadie moved in front of David and deflected the charge with her body. Simba backed off and circled the two, clearly surprised that his challenge was met. Constantly barking, he continued trying to make Cadie back down.

She would have none of it. But, unlike Simba, she made no sound.

She simply locked eyes. After several minutes, she'd had enough. Simba's bravado was getting old. She sat down as if to say, "When you're done, we can talk. But, right now, you're boring me."

This challenge would not go unmet. He worked his way in, closer and closer, continuing to bark at her. Finally, when he came close to her, she did the most un-shepherd-like thing David had ever seen a dog do. She gave Simba a roundhouse with her right paw, connecting with the side of his head. Apparently, Simba had never experienced such a move either, as he literally stumbled and fell. Lying on the ground, he had the distinct look of "What just happened?"

Cadie went to him and stared down into his face, as if to say, "That's enough. Act your age."

With that, Simba got up and moved to her side. All pretense of fighting and bravado gone, the order was established. It was clear that they were going to get along.

Satisfied, David made the arrangements to take Simba home, keeping in mind that the second hurdle was Shelby. Would Simba be all right with her? Again, it was a no-go if he wasn't good with her. But David needn't have been worried. They hit it off right away. David lost no time heading to the park and starting the training exercises. Having Cadie there helped Simba pick up the routine very quickly. He would begin training him for search and rescue, and for therapy, right away.

Back at LifeCare, Mary and Cadie had become friends. With Cadie to encourage her, she had graduated from a wheelchair to a walker, and then from a walker to a cane. People all over the room stood and smiled as she led Mary back and forth over a set of therapy stairs.

"I wouldn't believe this change in Mary if I hadn't seen it myself," the center director said. "Cadie is working her magic all over the place, but I don't need to tell you that. I see her succeed where trained therapists have made little inroads."

"That's what angels do!" David replied, smiling hugely, as he and Cadie prepared to head home.

On the way back to his car, David's cell phone rang. A voice hard to recognize on the little speaker said, "Hello, is this David?"

"Yes, it is."

"This is Pastor Mike. Remember me? I heard you were an even bigger hit at Boston Baptist College than you were with the youth group here. Congratulations."

"Thanks."

"I was very impressed with the speech you gave at our church a few months ago and was wondering if you'd be willing to do it again at a symposium we're putting on. I'd like you to be one of our guest speakers."

"Me? Are you sure about that?"

"You hit a home run at both of these groups. You're really thinking out of the box, as far as doing God's work is concerned. I mean, using God's creatures for God's people—who wouldn't love that? I think it would be an inspiration if you'd agree to come talk about it."

"How large is the group?"

"Oh, a thousand or more."

David stopped walking; he stopped talking too.

"David?"

More silence.

"David, are you there?"

David cleared his throat. "Yes, I'm here," he said in a husky voice. "I was just trying to take that in. I guess I can do that. I'm really honored, but that's a lot of people."

"I understand. Talk it over with Hope, and get back to me. How about by Monday, okay?"

"I'll call you Monday morning. Bye."

This is going to be an interesting talk with Hope, David thought.

Soon after they discussed it, Hope came in with the mail, to find David sitting on the couch, a shepherd on each side of him. She smiled. "So, have you decided?"

"I'm having a bit of a problem wrapping my head around the fact that there will be a thousand-plus people there."

She raised an eyebrow. "You just remember that God started this in a small way, and He's grown it. Now you have an opportunity to reach all those hearts."

"I know … you're right. But still."

"Is there anything I can do to help you? Would you like me to be there with you?"

"Yes, I would. I'm going to need the moral support. And I'd like Shelby to be there too. I want her to bring Cadie out at just the right time."

The day of the symposium arrived, only to find David in a panic. Emerging from the bedroom, he called for Hope. "Honey, have you seen my pants?"

Hope came down the hallway and looked at David. Shirt, tie, socks … no pants. Trying not to laugh—too much—she touched his shoulder and said, "You mean the ones you have draped over your shoulder?"

"Yes, the ones I have on my shoulder." David looked dazed as he headed back to the bedroom.

Hope shook her head as she watched him walk away. "Are you leaving for the conference early?"

"I think I'm going to leave early for the conference."

"Is there an echo in here?" Hope asked herself softly.

David reemerged, with his pants on, and seemed ready to go. He was dressed at least. "An echo? What are you talking about?" David asked, and then he said, "Cadie and I are going to go early, so we can have some quiet time to get ready. I'll see you and Shelby at 3:00 p.m. We'll meet backstage, okay?"

"Okay. We'll see you there, sweetheart. I'm really proud of you."

Shelby ran to hug his neck. "Me too, Daddy."

David went outside, put Cadie in the car, got in, and drove off.

He pulled into the parking lot at the church, put Cadie on a lead, grabbed his speech, and headed inside. They familiarized themselves with the arrangement, then found a quiet place to rest and compose themselves.

A stagehand came in and approached him. "Mr. Hyler? I just wanted to let you know that there has been a small schedule change. It doesn't impact you, but we've added a very special speaker right after you. We found out that Pastor Fordham was attending, and we couldn't resist having him speak."

The stagehand walked out, and David followed him, with Cadie alongside. "Hey, wait a minute. Did you say Fordham?"

At that moment, Pastor Fordham himself came around the corner. He took a look at David, then glanced down at Cadie with disgust. "David, I see you're on the agenda today. I'm not sure what you think you are going to talk about, but keep this in mind. I will not tolerate the scripture being perverted to fit your view of God's creation. And I speak following you." Fordham spun on his heel and stalked off.

Clearly shaken, David returned to the ready room and collapsed into a chair.

Hope entered with Shelby, took one glance at his face, and ran over to him. "Honey, what's wrong?"

He didn't look up. "Who do I think I am?"

"What are you talking about?"

"Fordham's here." He gestured half-heartedly toward the door. "I just saw him in the hallway, and he can't wait to have Cadie and me for lunch."

"He's the one who's wrong, and you know it."

His head came up. "Do I? Do I really? Who am I to challenge a biblical scholar like Pastor Fordham? He's a top graduate from one of the most prominent seminaries on the planet, ministers to a church of thousands, and has a teaching ministry in at least sixty-five countries. And you say I'm the one who's right? Maybe he's right—this is nothing more than an ego trip I'm on."

Hope's eyes darkened with passion. "Stop it! You stop that right now! There's no ego about you with any of this. I know your heart, and so does everyone else. We see it every day in your actions—how you treat others, and how you treat Cadie."

She grabbed his speech from the table next to him and shook it in front of him. "You did the research. You know this better than anyone, and I don't care what credentials any of them have. Remember what your grandfather said: You've prepared yourself for the battle. Don't back down when it comes time to fight."

Another stagehand stuck her head in the door. "One minute, Mr. Hyler."

"I can't fight this. Besides, what if I'm wrong? It would be the biggest failure of my life. Yet again."

"That's the devil talking, David. God is with you and Cadie."

"No, really. I can't do this. I'm not going to embarrass you or Cadie or Shelby with this. I quit."

He stood to leave, but Hope grabbed his sleeve. "Don't you dare. We're counting on you, and, what's more important, God is counting on you. Fordham is simply a man, and he's wrong about this. You're the only one who can tell those people. I'm begging you: finish this for God, and quit worrying about us ... and about yourself."

The stagehand returned. "Mr. Hyler, it's time."

David turned back toward Hope and stared at her.

"Mr. Hyler, we have to go now."

"You two stay here with Cadie," he pleaded.

David started out of the room, feeling utterly defeated.

Hope tried to hand him his speech, but he waved it off. "Keep it. I'm not going to need it."

As David approached the stage, he heard the speaker saying, "Our next speaker will be David Hyler, who is here to talk about creative evangelism and his unique approach to spreading the gospel. He's clearly a man who thinks outside the box when it comes to serving God."

The man then looked over to ensure that David was standing in the wings. "And now, I'd like you to meet David Hyler."

There was applause, but David didn't move.

The speaker again said, "Mr. David Hyler."

Finally, the stagehand nudged him forward. "Go, go."

David walked slowly to the podium, approaching it as if it were the gallows and completely unaware of what was going on behind him.

Meanwhile, as the door closed upon David's exit, Hope had turned to Shelby. "Come on, sweetie, we need to pray for Daddy right now. You too, Cadie."

Hope and Shelby finished their prayer.

Cadie moved to the door and started pawing at it.

"Cadie, no," Hope said.

Cadie stopped but continued to sit there. A moment later, she began whining.

Shelby said, "Mom, she needs Daddy."

Hope smiled at her. "No, honey, Daddy needs *her,* and she knows it."

The presentations were being carried throughout the speakers of the church's sound system. So, Hope clearly heard David's introduction, as well as the audience's reception. When she heard David's voice, so soft that he could barely be heard, she became concerned. And Cadie stopped whining. Hope then heard him say, "Ladies and gentlemen, I had a speech prepared, but … well, I can't use it." Hope became alarmed.

At that moment, the stagehand opened the door. "Ladies, can I get you anything?" In an instant, the perfect storm erupted as Cadie bolted past her.

"Cadie! No!" Hope practically yelled. Turning to Shelby, she said, "Shelby, come on!" Without waiting for a response, Hope ran into the hall, calling for Cadie. Chasing a dog while wearing high heels was not exactly what she'd planned for this day.

Oblivious to the events with Cadie, David gripped the podium tightly. "For the past few years, I've been doing what I believed was right for God, simply serving Him by serving His people. I've always believed God works through His creation to help us. But, today, I was told by a prominent spiritual leader that all I've done is pervert scripture for my own selfish desires."

Pastor Fordham, seated in the front row, nodded in agreement with the statement. He looked very smug as murmurs began to grow throughout the audience.

Meanwhile, elsewhere in the building, Cadie was following David's scent. She made quick work of tracking David through what seemed to be a cavernous building, with turns everywhere. And then, she heard his voice as she came into the wings, and she stopped. In the same instant, Hope and Shelby rounded the corner. They came up behind Cadie, and they also stopped. Cadie, totally focused on David, ignored them as she sat in the doorway. Cadie, motionless, stared at him, as if trying to quietly get his attention.

Still oblivious, David continued. "No one should be in a position like this, simply for following God's teachings."

Then, David saw his family. He looked at the three of them but ignored them. Tears glistened on Shelby's cheeks, and Hope's eyes pleaded with him. Hearing the resignation in his voice was unbearable. It seemed he was lost, giving up. The pause he was taking was dragging out far too long.

Meanwhile, Cadie remained motionless. She was backlit by the sunlight. Once referred to as an angel in a fur coat, that was exactly what she looked like in that moment. It was then that David noticed her. And something changed in him. He stiffened his spine and stood up straight. Maybe he would go down and be humiliated, but he was ready for the battle—and he wouldn't give up without the fight. Enough of this.

Turning his attention back to the crowd, he leaned toward the microphone. Speaking loudly and confidently, he stated simply, "No one!"

Buoyed with a sense of confidence that could only be infused by an angel, David continued. "Let me tell you a story of another who was unwanted. Someone who spent time in prison for a crime she didn't commit; someone who came from a situation of horrendous abuse. She was locked in the back room of a house, and food was thrown in at her. She wasn't allowed to leave for two years!"

Pastor Fordham's face darkened, and a frown furrowed his forehead.

David ignored him. As he'd done for the youth group, David painted a picture with words for this audience, to help them visualize the situation the dog had been in.

"Darkness gives way to a faint light filtered through tattered curtains, the same ones you see every day. They're a dingy reminder that the new day is already filled with emptiness. Like all the past ones have been. Like all the rest are likely to be. Hours upon hours of nothing. Darkness at times. Yelling at times. Pain most of the time—either from mental abuse or physical torture. Strange sounds and smells most of the time too. But, all the time, there is fear and loneliness. This is not what life should be. Or is it?

"Then, a noise. Footsteps? Yes! Someone's coming! Do you dare to hope? The sound grows louder. Yes, someone's coming! The footsteps are distinct now! But … will this be the jailer?

"The door opens. Yes, you realize with dismay, it's the jailer. Food is thrown into the room. Just like every other time. And then, the jailer is gone. Your faint hope lies dashed on the floor, amid the spilled food and accumulating piles of waste. No one ever stops to clean up the mess that's become your home for the past two years. Why should they? You're worthless. Your cries go unanswered.

"Until, one day, someone new comes. This person heard your cries. He gives you, a prisoner, the gift of freedom. But it's hard to grasp, much less appreciate, a concept that you'd never, ever known before. A gift? The gift of freedom? What did you do to earn it? You're worthless … aren't you?"

He paused his story. "Can you relate to this? Have you ever been hurt by someone you cared about? Praised one minute and beaten down the next? Have you ever been hugged, only to be hit or yelled at when all you wanted was another hug? Have you ever wondered if you were loved? Have you ever felt lost, forgotten, worthless?"

David was on a roll. The audience was silent, clearly wanting to know more.

He thundered away. "Have you ever given up hope for a future? If you can answer yes to any of these questions, then you can identify, at least in part, with my friend in the story."

David continued to recite the story from memory.

"Apparently, this idea of freedom would be harder for you to understand than anyone could have guessed. Because, after two more years, years filled with compassion and help for you, 'the forgotten prisoner,' all hope of a real home has faded. You failed at six attempted adoptions, more than anyone else of your kind. You have no confidence in yourself, and you still live in fear. You're now cared for, your room is clean and bright, the smells are gone ... but you're also unadoptable. Unwanted. Unable to fit in. These are now the words used to describe a life that once held such promise. These are the words used to describe one of God's creations: Unadoptable. Unwanted.

"Your physical needs are met, your health is now good, but, deep inside, you long for more. You know you were made for more than just existing. You've been saved, but you're not serving. How can you? Adults don't want anything to do with you. You're not even allowed around small children. But you know, in your heart, that you can make a difference. You just need a little help.

"Then, one day, someone else comes along. This person is different from all the others. He's not afraid of you. He looks into your eyes and sees the beauty within you. He senses the promise locked away deep inside. What seemed like forever was only mere seconds, but, in that time, he decides he wants you to be his friend, and he wants to be yours. From that moment on, your life and his are forever changed. He has accepted you as one of his own, and you have accepted him into your life. You're partners about to embark on a journey. The darkness, fear, and loneliness are now distant memories of a forgotten past. Hope is now reality.

"So, that's my friend's story. But what does it have to do with creative evangelism? We all have a calling. In Matthew chapter 28, Jesus told his disciples, 'Go and make disciples of all nations, baptizing them in the name of the Father and of the Son and of the Holy Spirit, and teaching them to obey everything I have commanded you. And surely I am with you always, to the very end of the age.'

"Did you read yourself into this story, with Jesus being the one who came to release you from your prison? That's how my friend helps me tell the good news. If we're looking for a way to serve, sometimes it takes a helper, a friend, to come alongside and encourage us. Or, maybe we can be that encourager for someone else." David lifted his chin, and his voice gained even more strength. "In fact, let me bring my helper out now."

He snapped his fingers, and Cadie walked confidently through the heart of the crowd, straight to his side, and sat next to him. There was an audible reaction—a gasp, some murmurs, perhaps a laugh or two. "This is Cadie. As you can plainly see, she is a German shepherd. She's also an animal-assistance therapy dog. She works with children, the elderly, anyone who needs help, anyone who needs love."

Thunderous applause broke out. The senior pastor, sitting next to Fordham, nudged him, nodding in agreement.

David continued. "She came from a place of tremendous abuse, but, through love and patience, she's overcome her past to serve others. Just as Paul had Barnabas, and each of the early missionaries had a partner, each of you needs a partner to help you meet your calling in the Lord. Ask God what He thinks. Ask Him for help. But be prepared to accept the answer God sends you—regardless of what it is or how He sends it! You see, I asked God for help, and He sent me a partner. In fact, my partner is the one from the story, and, as I'm sure you've guessed, it's a true story."

David put a hand on her head. "Cadie has come from a situation horrendous abuse. Believe me, in my story, I gave you only a glimpse into her former world. Today, she's awesome with kids. She loves to help calm their fears at the doctor's office and help them learn to read in school. She helps me show people how our canine friends can aid those with special needs. She's even been featured on TV, and I consider her the 'poster child' for how love and compassion can make adoptions work.

"Officially, she works with me as an animal-assistance therapy dog specializing in children. Something no one ever dreamed she could do. In fact, she wasn't supposed to be placed in a home with small children, much less work with them! But 'with God, all things are' … well … you know the rest of the verse. What makes her truly special is that she helps me tell people about God. After all, *dog* spelled backwards is *g-o-d*—God. And His story, for her, has turned out to be better than any a playwright could have ever penned. After all, who would have dreamed that my partner for telling the greatest story would be a German shepherd nobody wanted?"

David looked out over the audience, and smiled. "Okay, I can see it in your faces. You're wondering, *How does she help him tell people about God?* Simple. Most everyone loves a well-behaved dog. People stop and ask to pet her. They talk about dogs they've had in the past. They talk about themselves. They ask about her. In other words, they open the door. I don't have to. Then, I tell her story, and before you know it, the gospel is being shared. The message of rescue, salvation, hope, and love is being passed on. Just look at how bleak her future was, for years. Yet, with love and respect, she blossomed. She's helped impact young lives.

"As I said a while ago, she's a living example of how salvation works in our own lives, with the Great Shepherd, Jesus Christ, coming alongside and encouraging us, giving us freedom from our prison of sin. How many of us can identify with that? Her story brings people closer, and they become more receptive to hearing the gospel. Or, put it this way: we humans are visual creatures, and she's a great visual aid!

"And all this happens while they're petting a dog no one wanted and who had been judged to be worthless.

"So, I challenge you to open your mind. The more people hear and see examples from your own life, the greater your testimony. And never assume you have to fit into a cookie-cutter mold of evangelism. God has given each of us gifts ... use the gifts He's given you! Be creative. He is, so why shouldn't you be too? Look at Cadie. Who would have thought a dog could help witness? But I would say to you, Why not? She's part of His creation too. Psalm 8:6 says, 'He put everything under our feet.' So, don't overlook the opportunities out there to help you share Christ!"

David stopped now and tried to read the audience's faces. Was he through? He looked at Hope, standing in the door, backlit by the light, tears glistening in her eyes. *Almost done ... but not quite,* he decided. He saw a little girl in the front row, sitting in a wheelchair. Her father was holding up her head. She was listening and trying to smile. How had he missed seeing her before now?

He looked down. He might have missed her, but Cadie hadn't. She was totally focused on this little girl, as if she were the only person in an audience of more than a thousand people. David had come to recognize that look—a look that said, "I need to help that person." He had also come to trust his angel in a fur coat. He looked back at the little girl and then quietly said to Cadie, "Go ahead, girl, it's all right."

Immediately, Cadie rose and walked down the stairs at the front of the stage. Focused only on the little girl, she went right to her, sat down next to her, and positioned her head under the hands of the special-needs child.

The girl, though unable to make a sound, was clearly delighted. Every eye in the room, even the eyes of Pastor Fordham, were now on Cadie, and the little girl who was responding with pure joy. It was another miracle, a moment of magic.

David looked on, with a sense of pride and wonderment at what God was doing for the little girl through his so-called unwanted dog. He asked himself again if he was through and decided that he was. He felt spent. He had said what was in his heart, what he felt God had placed in his heart, and he would stand by it.

"That's our story. But let me close by saying that no one—and I mean *no one*—should ever be or feel unwanted." David looked directly at Pastor Fordham as he drilled home his final point. "Especially those who have been paid for by the death and resurrection of our Lord, Jesus Christ."

He turned from the podium to go offstage. His heart stopped when there was no response. In the next instant, a polite round of applause started. To his amazement, it built until it became a standing ovation.

In the crowd, Pastor Fordham applauded as well, though not enthusiastically. When people around him rose, he got up, probably so as not to call attention to himself. It appeared to David that he was surprised at the impact David's talk had on the crowd. These were not laypeople, these were his peers—pastors and active workers in the churches. He surveyed the faces. This was not a courtesy response. He had really touched these people. But what of Fordham? Best not to wait and find out. David began looking for an exit.

Just then, the announcer said, "And now, ladies and gentlemen, a man who needs no introduction. From North Carolina, Pastor John Carson Fordham."

David saw Fordham hurry to the podium. He wasn't about to let David and his family get away before he could say something. Not now. Not after that display. David had no desire to listen to Fordham speak. He turned to Hope and ushered the family along to the side exit. Quietly, he whispered to Hope, "Let's get out of here ..." Cadie joined him as they headed for the door.

"Mr. Hyler, *wait!*" Pastor Fordham's voice boomed throughout the auditorium.

David froze. The building had been silenced by the thunderous command. This was the last thing he wanted, to have to stand here and be publicly humiliated. But to leave now would make it worse. He steeled himself.

"David was very much a gentleman," Fordham said from the podium. "He refrained from telling you, or even suggesting, that the spiritual leader who accused him of perverting the scriptures was none other than me."

A shocked murmur rippled through the audience.

"I was quite prepared to come up here following his talk and publicly ridicule him for what I considered to be very inappropriate behavior. I was so sure bringing that dog into a church environment was absolutely wrong. But that was because I hadn't seen the results. I practically drove him from my church and my community for the same reason." He paused. "This is very hard for me—"

He stood there a moment, seemingly trying to collect himself. "But I get it now. I was wrong." He looked at David. "Thank you. I owe you an apology. Not a private one that would spare me the embarrassment I feel, but a public one, as public as I made it for you. It is one I deliver to you now, and will deliver again from my own pulpit when I get home."

He turned back to the podium. "Obviously, this is not what I intended to speak about, but, perhaps, I have had my eyes opened to something better to talk about. Please don't think I am bragging if I tell you that I know my reputation. I know I am looked upon as something of an expert, a teacher, a leader of my flock—and even as having a ministry that transcends that flock. It is an honor to be held in that high regard, but it comes with a price. From such a platform, people tend to take what you say as an absolute. They do so even if you are wrong."

He looked down, as if weighing his words. "The danger with being an expert and a teacher is that you … think … you … know. And when you know it all, you cease to learn. You cease to grow. I was so sure bringing that dog into a church environment was inappropriate that I didn't for one moment look to see what David was accomplishing. I see now that changing times do require considering new ways to reach out and that 'the way we have always done it' may not be the only way."

He smiled a genuine smile. "You see, I watched you as you listened to him, and I saw the effect that he had on you. Every one of you was drawn in by his words. The story of the dog touched you in a very real place where you want to go when you really understand. Jesus used parables when He taught, and David understood that lesson when he spoke to you today."

He met David's gaze straight on. "David, I came here today to teach. I should have come to learn. Thank you for teaching me."

The members of the audience jumped to their feet as one, applauding. The pastor walked across the stage to shake David's hand, then knelt to rub Cadie on the head. She seemed to accept it as her due.

It took a while for the auditorium to clear, as it seemed everyone wanted to meet David and Cadie, to shake his hand and congratulate him. Beside him, Pastor Fordham was also fielding well-wishes, people congratulating him on being big enough to admit when he was wrong.

David was astonished when he heard Pastor Fordham tell one person, "A number of people have told me that David changed some hearts here today, and I can see that's true. Perhaps mine was the one that needed the change the most."

Hope came up to David. Tears glistened on her cheeks as she said, "I can't tell you how proud I am."

"Be proud of God. He did it. Not me."

Cadie stood by his side and looked at him, her eyes shining as brightly as David had ever seen them.

He smiled down at her. "C'mon, girl. Let's go home."

EPILOGUE

This journey was about one man, one dog, and a powerful God who worked through both of them to accomplish miracles in their own lives and the lives of others. You see, journeys do begin one step at a time.

So, here we are, at the close of one journey and the beginning of many more—in both your life and mine, and with newfound confidence.

We all have the ability to reach out in love and acceptance; to make a difference in the world. How will you choose to make a difference in your own personal and unique way? Whatever and however you choose, just do it. The world needs you.

Jim (the author) and Cadie

ABOUT THE AUTHOR

Society is a reflection of the stories it tells itself through entertainment.
Are you happy with how society is going? No?
Then change the entertainment.

Author, filmmaker, speaker, and entertainment executive, Jim Huggins focuses on telling stories and telling them well in order to influence society in a positive manner. At a recent Hollywood summit, *Variety Entertainment* referred to Dr. Huggins as one of the "top entertainment chiefs" for faith and family film, TV, and digital media. Currently, he serves as the President and CEO of New Shepherd Films, an independent film production company producing faith and family entertainment for the mainstream market. He also serves as the head of New Shepherd

Entertainment, a faith and family promotional and marketing venture dedicated to being a resource to independent producers, and is a member of the Board of Advisors for Valorous TV, a network focused on bold and brave films, stories and reports of courage and uncommon valor.

With a BS in mathematics, Jim began his career as an officer in the Air Force in 1984. After a string of successes that ultimately took him to the Pentagon, he volunteered for a selectively manned position at HQ US Central Command during Operation Desert Storm and continued to serve in subsequent operations in the Middle East and northern Africa. He has received numerous awards, including the Defense Meritorious Service Medal, two Joint Service Commendation Medals, and the Air Force Commendation Medal.

Presented with unique opportunities to direct his talents toward innovative technology startup companies in the private sector, Jim moved from the Active Duty forces to the Reserves. Continued success propelled him upward, with ever-increasing responsibilities, where he excelled at a global level as part of a select management team between AMR and CSX, two of the world's largest transportation companies. Along the way, Jim earned his MS in engineering and PhD in engineering management, specializing in computer and software engineering.

Jim has taught a variety of disciplines at two major universities. He served as a professor of computer science at Campbell University, as well as an adjunct professor of aerospace studies for the Air Force, teaching Islamic Fundamentalism and The Laws of Armed Conflict at NC State University.

In 2006, Jim set his sights on the entertainment industry. Recognizing the need for family-friendly films and other entertainment products with a solid faith-based message, he turned his passion for storytelling into the driving force behind a new career. By 2009, Jim had become an award-winning stage actor, experienced director, and professionally trained TV/film actor. From this, came New Shepherd Films, an entertainment company dedicated to producing faith and family content specifically for the crossover audience.

By 2011, Jim and his team released their first film, *Footprints: Angels*

Are Real—Some Even Have Fur. Based on the reviews, audience reactions, and an ever-increasing fan base, New Shepherd Films clearly hit the target.

Jim's desire to impact the culture around him as a storyteller, goes beyond movies—entertainment extends to books as well. To this end, Jim has become a published author, with two books in worldwide release and more in the queue! These efforts have resulted in Jim being awarded a doctor of divinity degree for his work in creative evangelism.

Jim and his wife, Leslee, their kids Emma, David, and Samuel, and their rescued German shepherd, Lily, are originally from North Carolina and today, they call Salem, Oregon, their home.

Angels are real. Some even have fur.

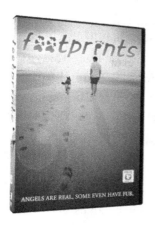

**#2 Amazon Best Seller –
available on DVD and download!**

Visit www.footprintsmovie.com and order your copy today.
Stay on top of what's happening…follow our journey at

facebook.com/footprintsmovie

"A wonderful story which features a young boy named David Hyler and the struggles he faces over the years into his adult years… As a man David cares for German Shepherds and when an abused one named Cadie comes into his life, in addition to a new wife named Hope, David has a chance to live the kind of life he longs for…the themes of this movie are great: forgiveness, loyalty, second chances, and love. Catch this one!"

- The DOVE Foundation

4+ EXEMPLARY!

"The story is one of a man who finds hope, love, and fulfillment in an unlikely place as he follows God's direction. "FOOTPRINTS" has a very strong Christian, moral worldview with references to forgiveness, hope, and love. The flashbacks are extremely well directed and acted. The jeopardy is intense...there's something clearly at stake, that is, David's survival and Cadie's survival...A strong entertaining, Christian story that is well worth watching. The movie tells a strong Christian story in a positive manner...wonderful message of faith in God's plan...well worth watching!"

- Dr. Ted Baehr

"There is much uncertainty in life these days. People are concerned about a great many things, and movies have always been an escape for us from the pressures of life. So we make the drive, buy the ticket, and for two hours we allow our head to get filled with stuff, much of it does nothing to encourage us. FOOTPRINTS is different. New Shepherd Films is different. You will feel the difference when you leave the theater...a wonderful story, the kind of story our troubled times needs more of."

- Bob Kemp, Renew America Magazine

"Multimillion dollar budgets for special effects can serve to draw crowds to Hollywood's latest blockbuster. A $20 million A-list actor or actress can nearly ensure that every theater seat will be filled on opening day. But writer and director Jim Huggins has utilized the third, and perhaps most important ingredient needed to make a good movie: A good, heartwarming storyline. "FOOTPRINTS" has a strong musical score, good lighting and editing, a tempo that doesn't drag, and solid acting punctuated by the heartwarming dogs themselves. Take the family, it's appropriate for all ages. It's so well done, that even a cat person will love it!"

- Daryl Madore, Times Record

A special word from German Shepherd Rescue of New England

"**FOOTPRINTS** is a compelling true story of the rescue of both people and animals. The lead K9 actor in this movie is an adopted GSRNE (German Shepherd Rescue of New England) dog, Rocket, whose canine personality comes shining through. In fact, most of the German Shepherds appearing in the film are rescued animals, reflecting the ideals of the producers. This is a Christian-produced movie; and Jim and Cadie's stories show the profound effects each had on the other."

AUDIENCE REACTIONS

- "This movie will change your life."
- "We saw the movie. I found it to be very touching as did my boy. When the little boy in the film was told his mother was not coming home, Ricky climbed into my lap and started hugging me and fidgeting at the same time. I knew the movie got to him so I asked him what the problem was. He told me he was sad for **ME**! I asked why and he said because **MY** mommy had died. My jaw dropped to the ground. I was amazed to realize how much empathy my little boy has. It was incredible. Thanks. **Your movie helped me to realize something about my son that surprised the heck out of me.**"
- "This is a wonderful movie! I received my DVD Saturday and watched it with my parents Sunday! Such a strong message!"
- "Excellent! Can't wait to see it – *AGAIN!*"
- "We finished watching FOOTPRINTS last night. It is an incredible story. Great job!"
- "Just got my movies in the mail today and the whole family sat down and watched it!! Great job on this movie. The message is awesome!"
- "It's about time Hollywood steps up and recognizes good down home family values movies instead of blood, gore, sex, & violence. CONGRATULATIONS and keep up the GREAT work. Continue to spread the word!"

- "Jim has unbelievable instincts. He has been a source of inspiration, comfort, guidance, and light for me in my new discovery and appreciation of God."
- "A friend of mine just saw the film the other night and told me how amazing it was...she was RIGHT!"
- "Dawn and I went to the screening last night in Vermo nt. It was worth the two hour drive. They have done a fabulous job at telling a great story. It demonstrates that God can work though any channel."

ABOUT NEW SHEPHERD FILMS

People love stories. And we're visual creatures. That's why stories
told with pictures—motion pictures to be more precise—are
so effective at communicating a message. The only question
becomes "What message do you want to communicate?"

Founded in 2009, New Shepherd Films has quickly become a recognized
leader in Christian entertainment. In all our products, we strive to
tell true stories that are uplifting and inspiring, yet told with a level of
sophistication that appeals to the broadest audience possible and captures
the imaginations of all people, regardless of age or faith.

Our creative team is one of the most experienced and dynamic teams
around. In just our co-founders alone, Jim Huggins and Russell
Dougherty, we have over 50 years of combined experience overseeing
artistic and technical leaders from a wide range of backgrounds in film
and entertainment. New Shepherd Films is devoted to producing high-
quality, family entertainment with Christian-oriented themes based on
real life events. We want to entertain our audience with high-quality,
creative talent and technological capabilities while at the same time tell
true stories about God at work in everyday lives. Everyday. And do so with
films appeal to both children and adults without a heavy-handed approach
to presenting faith-based values.

Given the pace of our society...with all the demands, distractions, and
pressures we face every day...it's easy to lose sight of the fact that God

really does exist and that He's involved in our lives. Engaging stories are a great way to slow down and see the world around you from a different perspective!

And with more stories under development, New Shepherd Films promises to be here to stay.

Printed in the USA
CPSIA information can be obtained
at www.ICGtesting.com
LVHW052154070724
784866LV00019B/88

9 781480 880627